(Strategic Commandos)

Trained in guns and explosives,
international espionage, terrorism
and guerilla warfare.

STONE: Background, the Ivy League. Vietnam vet, master strategist with a computer's cunning. Talent: organizing death.

MYLES: Mr. Cool from the South Bronx with a Haitian heritage, ghetto guts and Vietnam memories. Expertise: weaponry.

LEAH: Training by Israeli Intelligence. Skills: can dismantle a bomb, pilot a fighter jet, speak six languages. Specialty: sex.

LUCKY: Miami Cuban, anti-Castro terrorist with a passion for money, a hunger for women. Craft: making bombs.

ROD: Outback Aussie—big, bigoted, with Vietnam battle smarts. Operations area: the Jungle.

S-COM

Small private army
for hire. Terms: nego-
tiable. Payment in advance.

Books by Steve White

S-COM #1: Terror in Turin
S-COM #2: Stars and Swastikas

Published by
WARNER BOOKS

S-COM

#1

TERROR IN TURIN

STEVE WHITE

WARNER BOOKS

A Warner Communications Company

WARNER BOOKS EDITION

Warner Books, Inc., 75 Rockefeller Plaza, New York, N.Y. 10019

A Warner Communications Company

Printed in the United States of America

First Printing: October, 1981

10 9 8 7 6 5 4 3 2 1

S-COM

#1

TERROR IN TURIN

CHAPTER 1

The day was hot and the scene familiar to any visitor to Italy as hundreds jammed the steamy Turin Post Office with bills to pay, birthday cards to send, love letters to mail. The quiet of the waiting mixed with the buzz of impatience, although Italians long ago accustomed themselves to the tardiness of their government's lazily bureaucratic ways. Some dozed on line. Others read. Many chatted happily with their neighbors. A few, the bolder young ones, tried to strike up love affairs. It was just another calm Turin afternoon. Until the bomb ripped through the post office.

There was no warning. The bomb's frightening roar arrived unannounced. The post office, just seconds ago a cheerful community stopping-off place, collapsed in splinters. Dozens were dead; many, many more were maimed as the bomb's fury indiscriminately tore apart the building's masonry as well as arms, legs, and still more vital parts of human bodies. But no one, despite the spreading sea of destruction and carnage, looked shocked.

Italy was awash with terrorism. Bombings, shootings, and kidnappings were prominently featured in the terrorists' bag of black tricks. Violence was commonplace; nobody was safe. The rich, the poor, even the politically popular and powerful fell fatal victims to Italy's engulfing political violence. Ask the family of former Premier Aldo Moro. The Red Brigades proudly dumped Moro's bullet-ridden corpse on a bustling Rome street and publicly crowed that Moro's would not be the last Red Brigade murder. He was not. Hundreds and thousands more had already been killed in the wave of violence.

Italians, by now, had resigned themselves to living—and dying—with terrorism. It was an inextricable part of the fabric of the land. Nothing, no police or government step, had been able to curb the numbing explosion of Italy's home-grown agonies. When right-wing neo-Fascists blew up the Bologna train station and killed eighty-six people, a deadly response from the left was sure to come. It came today in Turin.

"Dammit," Stone Williams shouted at the bulletin on the late-night news which brought the horrifying details of the Turin massacre. For the moment, Stone was safe from the roar of bombs and an ocean removed from the eerie screams of the wounded as he sipped Scotch and intently watched television in his penthouse apartment on New York's Upper Eastside. But Stone, with his razor-honed commando mind, was never far from destruction and death. Wordlessly, he saw body after body being carted out of the Turin Post Office. His climbing anger was pushed beyond the boiling point when the camera panned onto a little girl no more than seven years old, then closed in to reveal her delicate face, half of it sheared off by the explosives. That's when Stone abruptly burst from his apartment.

The Turin mess, he told himself as he jogged mechanically to Central Park for an evening run that would be brutal enough to knock the Italian images from his consciousness, is none of my business. The Italian police, tacitly at least, admit they are powerless to stem the tide of terrorism. No agency, not even the ruthlessly efficient S-COM band that Stone commands, could twist a tourniquet tight enough to stop the flow of Italian blood. Stone knew as well what every top-notch security professional says about Italy: Avoid it! That's good advice, Stone reminded himself, and tonight he would take it as the rhythmic pounding of his feet on Central Park's always-dying grass gradually rid his mind of thoughts of bombs and deaths. But not even the hypnotically lulling effect of jogging could permanently erase from Stone's memory the image of a little Italian girl whose battered face would always carry with it the scarred memories of a hot Turin afternoon. Nor would it erase Stone's anger; it could only submerge his ire.

"Got a quarter, man?"

The question shook Stone from his moody reflections on Italy. Central Park after dark is off-limits to the law-abiding millions of New York; the night is when junkies and muggers stake their unchallenged claim to supremacy. But when Stone's thoughts turn their blackest, his midnight jogs invariably lead him into the darkest corners of the park, where his challenge to the night people of the park is unspoken—but unmistakable. Most nights, however, the challenge went unanswered. Muggers are vicious, but few are stupid enough to fail to sense the barely bottled-up venom that prompted Stone to wander into this grassy combat zone. And of the few who failed to perceive the knife-edge of Stone's turbulent emotions, most were deterred by his appearance. Stone was not an especially tall man; his tape-measure halted a fraction of an inch below six feet two inches. Nor did his physique bulge with the muscles of body-builders. His were taut, compact muscles, the kind developed to perfection in swimming, jogging, and bicycling—the aerobic sports Stone had increasingly favored since his graduation from Yale and the end to his quarterbacking career that it marked. But no, it was not Stone's body that would have sent an alert mugger looking elsewhere for prey. It was his face: good-looking, but angular with a tight, thin-lipped mouth and pale blue eyes that sucked the environment inward but offered nothing in return. If eyes are the window to the soul, as Stone had read in countless plays and poems, he had no soul at all, for his eyes offered a peek at nothing within, except a hard coolness. Those who knew Stone well, like his morals and philosophy teacher at Yale, Professor Worthington, insisted the evidence of the eyes was errant. But no night person of the park could be privy to their speculations about

Stone's true psyche. A mugger would see only the harsh hardness, and it was enough to stop the advances of all but the most foolhardy.

This mugger fell into the last clump, the foolhardy.

Ignore the question, Stone's mind begged. Just keep on jogging. One burst of speed would have put Stone well beyond the mugger's reach, but the little Turin girl, and how much she had suffered and would suffer because of criminal violence, flickered before Stone's eyes. He should have kept moving at his brisk pace. But Stone stopped to face his questioner.

"I said, got a quarter?" the mugger hissed.

"Nope," Stone nonchalantly replied. It was the truth. When jogging, Stone carried only two dimes for emergency phone calls; the coins were taped to the tongues of his sneakers, but Stone was not about to hand over his twenty cents. " 'Fraid not, buddy."

Stone tried to study the man's face, but shadows swallowed up his features. Then Stone glimpsed the knife, a hideous stiletto with a gleaming seven-inch blade.

"Think again, turkey, 'cause you know what they say: Your money or your life, mothafucker."

The blade flashed at Stone's stomach. The mugger's move was practiced and sure. Stone's was surer and swifter. One of his hands grabbed the mugger's wrist; the other took his elbow. Before an observer could have counted to two, Stone heard the snap. Exactly midway between the man's elbow and wrist, his arm broke. The knife floated harmlessly to the grass as pain seared through the mugger's every nerve-ending. But the man's lucky day it was not. Stone's foot—soaring at a speed once clocked at 52 miles per hour by a radar gun in the Fifth Avenue Tae Kwon Do studio he sometimes visited—smacked sharply against the mugger's face. The sound of a nose flattening and of teeth shattering followed. The man's anguished and pained screams interrupted the stillness of the night. Then, and this could be counted only as a miracle by crime-weary New Yorkers, another sound filled the air—the howl of a police siren as a pair of the City's finest descended on Stone and the bitterly demoralized and disarmed would-be mugger.

Not surprising, Stone thought acidly as one cop pointed his revolver at Stone. "Hands up, asshole," the cop said and the other rushed to aid the "victim."

Stone's placid recital of the facts, plus the cop's careful scrutiny of his driver's license—retrieved from yet another sneaker pocket—won him his release . . . and the mugger a well-deserved trip to the local precinct house.

Jesus, Stone thought as he reversed his jogging course and headed home for a night's sleep. Jesus, what a horrible day.

But many, many more such days would mark Stone Williams's calendar.

Back in Turin, Salvatore DiGrazia was well aware of the advice of security professionals and their unqualified warnings to steer clear of Italian soil. Fine as that advice is, DiGrazia knew he would never take it. Although fearful of the rampant disorder and murderous terrorism that pervaded his homeland, DiGrazia steadfastly remained in Italy. The nation, its rich past and sensual present, was his love. Not his biggest love; that title belonged to his gorgeous twenty-year-old daughter, Maria. But Italy ran a solid third in DiGrazia's affections, topped only by Maria and, in second place, DiGrazia's thriving automobile-manufacturing firm, Especiale. DiGrazia-made cars are sleek, fast, beautiful, and internationally admired for their continental charm. Maria fares every bit as well when it comes to earning admiration—her stunning good looks, grace, and an unmistakable air of unaffected wholesomeness see to that.

It was at lunch with Maria that DiGrazia first learned of the explosion at the Turin Post Office and of the mounting body count. "My God," DiGrazia groaned when the waiter brought him the news flash. But DiGrazia, a self-made man whose belief in himself and in his Italy could not be shaken, indulged not long in shocked pity. With Maria in tow, he rushed from his espresso to his factory and immediately issued orders that the Especiale staff doctor and nurse be driven to the crumbled post office to aid the injured. That was followed by a command to his factory workers to shut down production for the afternoon—despite a growing backlog of orders for the ever-in-demand Especiale automobiles—and to make themselves useful at the bomb site. "Help dig through the rubble," DiGrazia commanded over the PA system. He was confident that every one of his one-hundred workers would do just that; they knew DiGrazia himself would be there helping, too.

The scene DiGrazia saw at the post office was no different from the one Stone Williams saw a continent away. Except that Stone's sights were limited to what his television brought him. The blood, suffering, and pain were viscerally more real to DiGrazia in Turin as he lifted boards and bricks and, sadly, occasionally discovered a mangled body beneath. But maybe, he sorrowfully thought, maybe they are the lucky ones. At least they are dead.

A widower, whose wife died during the birth of his cherished Maria, DiGrazia was no stranger to suffering. As a Resistance fighter during World War II, DiGrazia—a small but confidently powerful man—struggled to free Italy from the sweeping tyrannies of Mussolini's Fascist Brown Shirts and to keep alive the Jews singled out for monstrous deaths by Hitler's Gestapo. Often enough DiGrazia's underground efforts paid dividends in lives saved. Just as often, however, the efforts failed in the face of the immensely superior firepower and might of the combined German and Italian armies. But DiGrazia never wavered in his determination to do what he thought was right, even when this dedication put his own life in jeopardy.

With the expulsion of the Fascists following their defeat by the Allies, DiGrazia—ever the optimist—had looked forward to decades of cheerful and peaceful rebuilding of his nation. But a series of unstable governments—there have been over thirty ruling factions in Italian politics since World War II—coupled with a beleaguered economy and a galloping inflation rate are the prescription for national unhappiness and turmoil. The Italian terrorists of the left, the right, and sometimes the center have filled that prescription with guns, bombs, and deaths. But the day's terror in Turin notwithstanding, DiGrazia's resolve remained firm.

"Do what is right, and *only* what is right" read the placard behind DiGrazia's desk at Especiale. For him, this was no meaningless homily. His employees, paid the highest wages in Italy's automobile industry, could attest to that. So could their families, who enjoyed Especiale-provided free medical care and university scholarships for any son or daughter of an Especiale employee who gained admission to a college. DiGrazia's Especiale might not be a worker's paradise, but he persisted in doing everything he could, everything that was right, to make it one.

"It is days like yesterday," DiGrazia confided the morning after the post office explosion, to his secretary, Sophia Giacomo, "that make me wonder why I stay in this country. For myself, I've no worries. But for Maria . . ." DiGrazia's voice trailed off. The horror he felt whenever he coupled the thoughts of his smiling Maria and terrorism was simply too great.

For six years, Sophia had served DiGrazia as his personal secretary, and in this unique case it was neither a cliché nor an exaggeration to say she was part of the DiGrazia family. Turin's gossips had linked the darkly sensual Sophia and DiGrazia in romantic ways, but they are wrong. To DiGrazia she was a second daughter. And Sophia, for her part, was unswerving in her loyalty to DiGrazia and in her deep concern for him, his daughter, and Especiale.

"Perhaps"—DiGrazia picked up the trail of his thoughts—"it might be better to send Maria away until the troubles are over. But when will they end? And how?"

It was better, Sophia knew, to let Salvatore DiGrazia ramble along in his thoughts when they turned this shade of gloom. But this morning, a new, scary thought struck her. "Savatore, shouldn't Maria have bodyguards? She'll never leave you and Italy; she's said that before and you know she means it. But how many of Fiat's Agnellis have been kidnapped? How many have been killed? A dozen? More? Maria, without guards, is an easy target. Perhaps I am speaking out of turn, but—"

"No, Sophia, you are not," DiGrazia interrupted. The tormented expression on his face palpably illustrated the rightness of Sophia's fears. "How could I have forgotten?"

But DiGrazia's forgetfulness in this matter was no mystery. His love for Maria was immense; so was his sometimes single-minded optimism about Italy. That Maria might prove to be a tasty target for terrorist kidnappers was precisely the sort of dank thought DiGrazia denied himself—until, that is, explosives leveled the Turin Post Office.

Within hours and despite Maria's protests, Sophia had secured for her round-the-clock protection. The instructions from DiGrazia were clear: Two armed guards were always to accompany Maria. That, insisted the firm which provided the guards within two hours of Sophia's call, would prove ample to keep the young lady out of harm's way. "She will be protected against any threat. You have our promise," the firm's owner had guaranteed, and DiGrazia happily took him at his word.

Where he himself was concerned, however, not the reports of recent Turin kidnappings—four during the past month—or even the worries of Sophia could prod DiGrazia into agreeing to personal bodyguards. "I survived Hitler and Mussolini. I can survive the Red Brigades, the Armed Revolutionary Nuclei, and whatever else these violent fools create," DiGrazia said and closed the conversation.

"The Seventh Mao Force," Stone snarled as he carefully measured out exactly six tablespoonfuls of fresh French roast coffee into his Krups grinder and whirred the beans into a fine grind. Breakfast was the meal Stone treasured. Every day, his mornings started with two croissants, Knott's Berry Farm marmalade from California, and four cups of strong coffee that he drip brewed using water heated to precisely 196 degrees. But this morning not even his orderly breakfast routine could shake Turin from his mind, and now a news bulletin reported who took credit for the post office bombing. "Credit" is how terrorists invariably put it; Stone Williams saw only blame. He's personally witnessed too many deaths in actions that terrorists later brag about. But this group, the Seventh Mao Force, was a new one to Stone. It's a far-left group, Stone could tell by the reference to the Chinese leader Mao, and probably—in keeping with Mao's philosophy—dedicated to fomenting an immediate worldwide revolution. The jangling of his unlisted, private telephone broke Stone's speculative train of thought.

"Hello, Stone. This is Leah."

"What do you know about the Seventh Mao Force," Stone—never one to chitchat even with good friends like Leah Aviv—hastily responded.

"I see you're keeping abreast with Turin," said Leah, S-COM's only female member and, as an Israeli and a former staffer in that nation's intelligence apparatus, a keen source of up-to-date scoops on worldwide terrorism. "But nobody knows much about this outfit. It's much smaller than the Red Brigades, my sources report, but it supposedly went far underground after Aldo Moro's marder in 1978. No connection with Moro's death; that's a piece of Red Brigade work. That's the puzzle. Who is the Seventh Mao Force? What is its goal? Absolutely nobody knows. Italian anti-terrorist police units are no help. Ever since the Armed Revolutionary Nuclei killed Judge Mario Amato in Rome—just when his investigations into their right-wing shenanigans were paying off—the police have made self-protection their first priority. That's the word I get, at least—"

"—there are no signs to the contrary," Stone, fully in tune and in agreement with Leah's judgment, completed her sentence. "Right now, Leah, it's no official concern of ours. But keep me posted . . . for the files."

With that, Stone halted their conversation. There were no hard facts and, much as Stone enjoyed Leah's company, he wanted to spare himself a fruitless and exasperating rehashing of yesterday's explosion. This was one morning that was not starting out right. Stone cursed the Seventh Mao Force and, for consolation, brewed himself a fifth cup of coffee.

Which left Leah to wrestle with another puzzle: How did Stone Williams, the son of an old-line Philadelphia lawyer, become the leader of the world's most respected fighting platoon? Leah's own evolution was an uncurving tangled path that puzzled neither Leah nor Stone: from a pacifist Israeli into a member of that battling nation's armed forces and, just before her involvement in S-COM, an Israeli intelligence operative whose skills were so admired that she was dispatched everywhere Israel found itself in trouble, from the Munich Olympics to the raid on Entebbe. One terrorist bomb too many had raped Tel Aviv's streets. That day, school children—a busload of them—fell victim to Palestine Liberation Organization violence. That day, too, Leah swore to forever continue the fight against terrorism.

But Stone's path was more tangled. It began at Yale and, following his graduation with honors, saw Stone putting in two tours of duty in Vietnam. Enrollment at Harvard Law came next. But that was one sheepskin Stone never collected. He quit abruptly and in short order assumed the S-COM helm. That odyssey was to Leah—and to everybody else, and maybe Stone himself—an enigma. Still, Leah had to smile at her reflections. No matter how it came to pass, she was happy that Stone was S-COM's leader. Nobody else could have kept that band of five gifted warriors together for a single day, and Stone had done it for seven years. Besides, each mission revealed a little more about the personal motivations that led Stone to stand at S-COM's bow. And a new mission, Leah could sense, was in the very near future.

CHAPTER 2

"We did it! We did it!" Vincent Teresio's joy knew no bounds as he pranced about his dank Turin home, the second floor of an abandoned, boarded-up factory that numbered among the casualties inflicted by terrorist bombs. Only a shell remained, although Teresio called it home and the dark, scarred structure fit his personality to a tee.

DARE TO STRUGGLE / DARE TO WIN, one of Mao Zedong's favorite slogans, was proclaimed in red ink just beneath a poster of the late chairman and architect of China's Communist government. Mao's face did not smile; neither, despite his joy, did Teresio's. He had not permitted himself a smile since taking over the leadership of the Seventh Mao Force in the summer of 1978—"after the capitalist running dogs showed their true colors and abandoned our revolutionary ship" is how Teresio described that confused time. But enough "running dogs" bailed out of Italy's politically extreme splinter groups in those stomach-wrenching days of terrorist excesses to leave Teresio with hardly a ship to steer. Winter 1977 saw a cadre of about fifty hardcore, dedicated SMF members, and at least that many more reliable financial supporters who always had a fistful of cash ready to support the revolutionaries. But in the wake of Aldo Moro's murder, "the cowards revealed their colors and resumed their black-hearted capitalist pursuits," or so Teresio explained the SMF's recent history. These days,

Teresio counted no more than five SMF members, most inactive, and not a single financial supporter. Even the fifty dynamite sticks that Teresio used to lay waste to the post office—"to triumphantly announce the renaissance of the SMF"—had to be stolen in a midnight raid on a construction site. Black market prices for explosives were beyond his reach, and all that remained in the SMF's armory from the wealthier days were two Russian-made AK-47 automatic rifles and a couple of thousand rounds of ammunition.

Slim as those provisions were in the world of sophisticated terrorism, Teresio's plans were many. The demolition of the post office was only the first prong. There would be others.

"Gina, we've dared to struggle. We've blown up the post office and redeemed the name of the Seventh Mao Force. Now, as Mao preached, we must dare to win," Teresio intoned in the humorless voice adopted by all terrorists.

" 'Fear no sacrifice; surmount every obstacle to win,' " Gina Frugis, Teresio's SMF compatriot and sometimes girlfriend, matched his Mao quotation with another. "Well and good, Vincent. The SMF is known throughout Turin now. But Vin, we may fear no sacrifices, but our treasury's down to zip. Not a dollar. Not even a few lira for pasta tonight."

"So? We'll live off the land as Mao did."

"This is not rural China, Vincent. It's urban Turin."

"Big deal. We'll *steal* food for tonight, and we'll steal more than pasta. A bottle of vino, good bread, and fresh butter. This evening, we eat; and tonight, we embark on the second prong of the plan. And then tomorrow, when the SMF is even more widely known and feared, we execute the third prong. Bang-bang. Put it together, and within a week we've solved our cash-flow problem. Shit! Did I say that? 'Cash flow.' When they put their capitalist mark on you, they put it good."

Three years of economics study at the University of Turin indeed had forever colored Teresio's speech. "Sinister capitalisms," as he flogged himself, often invaded his talk. That was appropriate too, because while Teresio draped his ambitions in communist garb, his desires were immutably capitalistic. So was his grand plan.

"Everywhere, under every rock, tree, and pot, there's a terrorist. We," Dalla Albanese, Turin's police chief, declaimed to his assembled men, "are in charge of stopping it, but it continues unabated. Yesterday, the post office. Tomorrow, what? The police station itself?" Albanese's tone of voice underlined the resignation that permeated every cranny of his department. In the face of mounting civilian violence, where no uniform demarcated the sides and in fact the nature and allegiances of the sides remained impenetrably blurred, the Italian police—Albanese very much included—had thrown up its hands. Theirs was a surrender. Certainly, in the face of angry questions from newspaper and television reporters in the aftermath of the bloody demolition of the post office, Albanese's public posture was proud and his commitment to eradicating the Seventh Mao Force and their ilk was firm.

But even as the dust still settled at the post office, Albanese confided to his wife that retirement, on full pension, "is my number one priority." Catching terrorists he likened to exterminating the cockroaches that, despite floods of lethal pesticides, continued to call his home their own. "Poison one and, yes, it dies," Albanese explained sadly, "but there are ten more that escape the spray. Kill them, and the next day one hundred rise in their place as if by magic. That's the way it goes with terrorists. We make headway in putting the Red Brigades out of business. Half of them, maybe more, are rotting in jail. Others, fearing the heat, renounce terrorism. But, so what? The Red Brigades are gone. The Seventh Mao Force appears—as if by magic." With that, Albanese slumped into his pre-dinner nap. He dreamt of a retirement free of cockroaches and terrorists alike.

"Hmmm. Delicious," Gina giggled as she and Teresio hungrily gobbled stray goodies off the laden shelves of

Balducci's, Turin's most chic and best-stocked food store. Olives, cheese wedges, and cherries nabbed off the tops of handsomely crafted pastries disappeared down their throats as they roamed through the jammed-to-the-rafters aisles.

"Try this," Teresio said, offering Gina a bite of the cannoli pastry he had liberated from an open tray.

"Yummy," she concurred.

"That's why I always shop at Balducci's," Teresio said, giggling at what for Vincent passed as a wildly comic joke.

Neither he nor Gina had ever shopped at Balducci's. The prices for the gourmet delicacies and exquisitely decorated edibles were too steep for most working Italians, let alone self-proclaimed revolutionaries whose last job was student. But sampling of wares is an Italian tradition, one the well-trained sales staff at Balducci's is taught early to encourage. A bite or two of anchovy might prompt a customer to purchase a pound; it will never result in the scream "Thief!"—not at Balducci's. The consequent commotion, the sales force knew, would unnerve the dignified, paying customers. Better to shrug off the snacking tours of Teresio and like-minded petty thieves than cause a stir. Even so, even at Balducci's, there were limits. That's a fact which Teresio discovered within thirty seconds of shoving a liter of pricey Moët White Star champagne under his shirt.

"Pardon me, sir. We've carts for use by our customers in carrying groceries to the cashier. There's no need to use your shirt," the assistant manager calmly remarked as his right hand—in stark contrast to the softness of his words—squeezed Teresio's shoulder sharply. "Here, let me help you to the cashier," the man concluded as his tightening grip steered Teresio directly toward an open cash register. "That will be all for you tonight, won't it?"

Teresio would have loved to pay for the champagne, but his pockets were empty even of bus fare and Gina's coffers, he knew, were no better stocked. What, Teresio wondered, would Mao do in this sort of fix? Would Mao have gotten into this mess in the first place? But Teresio's nervous thinking was interrupted by his forced arrival before the cashier, who, after listening to the assistant manager's whispered instructions, made himself busy ringing up Teresio's champagne purchase.

"With the tax, that's sixteen dollars and fifty cents, sir." The cashier extended his hand.

The store manager, his assistant, and the cashier all watched Teresio's every move as he began to dig feverishly through his pockets. But a bone-wrenching shriek broke their absorption with Teresio: "Help! My purse! It's been snatched," a well-dressed fat woman screamed before slumping in a faint to the floor.

Gina had waited for neither the alerting scream nor the faint. In one motion, she had tugged the heavy purse free of the porcine woman's careless hold and bolted, fast as a marathoner with snarling pit bulls on his tail, out of Balducci's front door.

Unaccustomed to such "affrontery," as the manager later characterized this breach in Balducci's decorum to the police, the trio of employees was shocked into momentary paralysis. So was Teresio—until he realized Gina was the culprit and that, amidst the growing confusion, he, too, could freely exit the store. Moët in hand, Teresio followed Gina's lead and scrambled out of Balducci's.

Within seconds, the employees, still uncertain of precisely what had transpired under Balducci's elegant roof, sprang into action. But utterly unprepared for such developments, theirs was an Italian rendition of the Keystone Cops. All three started to converge on the fallen woman, but they bumped resoundingly into one another and, on the rebound, the assistant manager opted to make chase after the fleeing purse snatcher. But by that time, Gina and Teresio were blocks away from Balducci's and Teresio was eager to celebrate this serendipitous "conquest of the capitalist pigs."

"Hold on, Gina. No need to run now. You know the Turin cops, they'll never catch us."

"Maybe tonight's their lucky night, Vincent. It's sure not yours. You damn near get us arrested. For what? A bottle of champagne? Incredible!" Gina angrily rebuked her revolutionary partner. "You always want to go one step too far. You *never* know when to stop!"

" 'The comrades,' Mao said," Teresio offered in explanation for the evening's hijinks, " 'must be helped to maintain the style of simple living.' "

"Amazing, Vincent. You stun me. Plain living? A bottle of champagne? You'll use Mao to justify anything," Gina retorted. "Remember, too, the chairman said, 'Be united, alert, and lively.' Alert you surely weren't, not with that guy staring over your shoulder when you slipped the wine into your shirt. Ah, Vincent," Gina exasperatedly ended her tirade.

Gina, a former art student, could not quite explain to herself her membership in the Seventh Mao Force. Her participation's start was harmless enough. Aghast at the deterioration of Italy's invaluable art works and architectural marvels in the face of mounting air pollution, Gina Frugis's radicalism began with peaceful protests against the befouling industries and automobiles that cause these ancient stones and canvasses quite literally to crumble into dust. But the destruction of Italy's art appeared unstoppable, and Gina, in climbing frustration, threw in her lot with Teresio and his SMF compatriots. Her goal had inalterably remained that of redirecting SMF's energies toward explicitly pro-art positions and actions, but somehow, she knew, that end seemed ever more distant. And Teresio's desire to put a "more muscular face on the revolution," as he put it, was bringing Gina no nearer her personal priorities. Violence had never been her style; she yearned to create, not destroy. Her days as an SMF member were numbered, Gina increasingly felt, and Teresio's clumsily bizarre antics at Balducci's that evening had not made her outlook more sanguine. Nor could she countenance the post office bombing, and she had refused each of Teresio's begged, shrieked, and muttered entreaties to join him. Even so, when she did feel a kinship to Teresio, it was an incredibly close feeling. That, too, Gina Frugis conceded to herself she could not explain. Unless, her curvaceously Mediterranean body shrugged, it was sex.

"Come here, Gina. First we celebrate. Then we fight," Teresio commanded his troop.

Although a bombed and burnt-out shell of a building, Teresio's accommodations included a bare mattress, where he sat and to which he beckoned Gina to come and share their "people's champagne." Glasses or not—and his hovel stocked not even plastic cups, to say nothing of the crystal goblets into which Moët under more normal circumstances customarily is poured—Teresio intended to fully enjoy this excellent vino.

"Wait," Gina laughed. "The purse, it was Signora Dalla Albanese's, the police chief's wife. That's who I robbed. Look, here's a photograph of the chief in uniform."

Teresio only glanced at the picture. "How much money did we get?"

"We? You mean, *me,*" Gina's Latin anger rose. "Not only did I save you from a trip, in the custody of the store manager, to visit Albanese under, shall we say, difficult circumstances, but *I* made us eating money for the next couple days."

"That you did," Teresio sneered, his male pride slighted by the piercing truth of her reportage of the night's events. "But," he cryptically remarked, "I had already planned on visiting Chief Albanese tonight. Perhaps we can return his wife's purse then. First, however," he grabbed Gina's fullness, "first, I say we celebrate *our* successes."

Maybe it was just sex, Gina thought as she acquiesced to Teresio's demand. For a Mao-quoting revolutionary, Teresio was unquestionably good and enduring in bed. No quickies for him; he'd taken to heart Mao's injunction to prepare for the long haul toward victory and applied it to every aspect of his life, bedtime play included. So Gina rapidly responded to his ardors. The revolutionary pair kissed passionately, with no thoughts of making revolution, just love. Teresio's hands moved with a delicate urgency to Gina's T-shirt; it slid easily off her body. A deft unhooking of her bra strap released her swelling breasts, and his lips rushed to meet them as his hands moved further down her ample body. Teresio's mouth enveloped Gina's puckering nipples, and as their mingling moans rose in intensity, both struggled free of their remaining clothes.

"I want you. Always," Teresio sighed contentedly between nibbles on Gina's breasts.

Gina replied wordlessly by guiding his bursting erection into her. His penetration was full and deep; her bucking, rhythmic response came in complete synchronization with his powerful thrusts. They hugged each other tighter as their movements grew less controlled, more spasmodic, faster. Teresio's tongue rammed into Gina's panting mouth and, like his erection, pushed deeper and deeper into her warmth. Their movements soon hit a frenzied sharpness. Small, orgasmic cries from Gina greeted Teresio's own rocking orgasm.

This was one time, when lovemaking concluded, that Teresio never quoted Chairman Mao. He was content merely to grunt with satisfaction. That was a feeling Gina gladly shared.

Minutes passed before Teresio roused himself to withdraw from her. As far as Gina was concerned at that moment, he could have remained in her forever. But Dalla Albanese—and Gina's earlier mocking—had crept into Teresio's mind and replaced the bliss he always felt when sex was good. He took another slug of champagne, handed the bottle to Gina to drain, and began sketching his plan for their late-night activities.

"What did I tell you? Nothing—that's all we can do against these thugs who run our town. Our town! It is theirs," Albanese rampaged when his wife told him of her purse snatching. A dutiful citizen, she offered to hurry to the police station to fill out the necessary forms—and in Italy there are dozens of papers to complete and sign even when an affair is as clean-cut as this one. But Albanese lashed out at her suggestion.

"And do what? Make a fool of me, that's what you'd

accomplish. Your purse, make no mistake, will never be recovered. The robber—a girl even!—will not be caught. I know my men. Put that idea out of your head. If the newspapers so much as hear a rumor that the police chief's own wife has been robbed, there'll be no end to the mockery. I can see the laughing editorials already. No, no! You cannot make an official report. I cannot control what goes on in Turin; but at least I can control what goes on in my own house."

Signora Albanese did not press the point. She knew the realities. Her husband etched them nightly for her with his ceaseless stories of rampant civil disorder and disrespect. All she could do is what she did: purr consolations and pour her husband a glass of the complimentary champagne Balducci's management had bestowed upon her in partial recompense for the night's unhappiness. The champagne, she observed, was a good grape, Moët. The irony escaped her and her husband.

It assuredly would not have eluded Gina Frugis, but she was then occupied with hearing Vincent Teresio's plan, one that very much involved the Albaneses, husband and wife.

"To make a name for the SMF, we've got to strike again. Hard and soon. The post office bombing got us started. But a second prong will make us better prepared when it is time to take the third, the biggest, step."

Gina was in the dark about this never-yet-described third prong of Teresio's master plan, but content with the evening's sex, she listened silently to Teresio's immediate agenda.

"To cite Mao, 'All the putatively powerful reactionaries are paper tigers. They are divorced from the people.' Who is the most grotesque paper tiger in Turin? Who, Gina?"

Gina shrugged noncommittally. Teresio, she was certain, would take delight in answering his own question.

"Dalla Albanese is," Teresio answered. "Some police chief. What a joke! The dumb fuck can't even protect his own wife from purse snatchers. When reporters are around, he pompously struts for them and mouths sanctimonious homilies about ridding Turin of crime and of what he benightedly calls terrorism. Yet he does nothing. That's good for us; we cannot deny it. But we know—Mao's writings have prepared us to understand—that the true terrorist is Albanese. It is his death warrant that the SMF issues and will presently execute. Dalla Albanese, that obscene paper tiger of a shit-eating and self-important bureaucrat, dies tonight."

"Aren't we pressing our luck, Vin? To strike again so soon after the post office bombing? Especially since we've already had a run-in with bad luck tonight," Gina said hesitatingly.

"But that luck turned good. We got a meal, a bottle, and ten bucks besides. It is Albanese whose luck has soured. The SMF is foreclosing his mortgage on life. Poof!"

Again, Gina paused. Although she did not admit it to Teresio, the deaths and injuries at the post office had sickened her. Could she stomach more killings? Were her ties to the SMF and Teresio that strong?

Teresio, perhaps unconsciously sensing her uncertainties, alertly brought her doubts to a standstill: "Break down the AK-47s, Gina," he barked. "There can be no slip-ups tonight. *Our* lives are on the line. Remember that! One goof and we die, and Albanese becomes the hero."

As Gina plunged into the preparatory activities, the urgency of her questions dimmed in importance. The feel of the amazingly light but shatteringly powerful AK-47s always thrilled her. Her pleasure in them, she mumly giggled to herself, was nearly sexual. The guns, she imagined as she tore them down to inspect every part, were gargantuan penises, ones that could—in response to a gentle command—transmit hundreds of semen bursts. A barely perceptible squeeze, that's all the AK-47 demanded to trigger its slamming message. But the AK-47, unlike a penis, was not designed for making babies. One of its quick chatters put an instant end to babies, children, adults, and anything else that dared to invade its path of remorseless bullets. But that, too, Gina smiled, is akin to a man's ready erection: Neither possesses a conscience.

"Our sleep, at least, cannot be robbed," Albanese said to his wife as the pair slid into bed. "Not with the twenty-four-hour guard I've ordered around our house. Here we are safe," he muttered just before dozing off into yet another dream of retirement's tranquillity. Signora Albanese swiftly joined him in sleep and dreamt her own dream of a life free of the worries Albanese's job brought. But for them their dreams were never to come true.

Outside the Albanese villa, Teresio and Gina made ready to execute the SMF death warrant. No police guards interfered with them. Unbeknownst to Albanese, his order requisitioning police protection for his home lay buried in the night-watch commander's paper piles. It would be days before anyone discovered the order, and fearful for his own job, the watch commander who made this eerie find hurriedly burned the evidence.

But Gina and Teresio knew nothing about the guards who were imagined by Albanese to be safeguarding his night's rest or about the black comedy of paper destruction that was played out at the police station. They knew only that this kill—their first using AK-47s or any kind of gun for that matter—looked simple enough.

"It's *too* easy, Vin," Gina cautioned, hoping perhaps to call a premature halt to this night's murderous work. "The street is empty. No lights are on. It's like they prepared the way for us. It's gotta be a fucking trap."

"Nope, it's just the Turin police," Teresio cynically—and accurately—analyzed. "Thinking is beyond them. Come on, let's see if the fool's left a window open for us."

Albanese had. His bathroom window always stood open, day and night, "a matter of personal hygiene," Albanese punctiliously explained to his wife. "The cold," he staunchly maintained, "kills germs." It did not. But tonight it would kill him.

The SMF duo crept through the open window, and following the rumble of Albanese's snore, they bumped in the dark against the door to the master bedroom, where the Albaneses slept. The jostling made a slight noise; it would have alerted a soft sleeper to intruders. The Albaneses slept soundly. They awoke only when Teresio hurled open the door and shrieked madly, "I have presents for both of you." With that he tossed Signora Albanese's pocketbook at the bed and, an instant later, let loose the unforgiving fire of his AK-47. His gun roared so loudly that Teresio did not notice that Gina's stood silently at her side; she had not even raised her gun to aim. And she thanked the darkness for shrouding the bleeding corpses. But, pitch black or not, her art student imagination forced her to picture the Albaneses as they lay dead in their bed. The picture she envisioned was not a pretty one. The real picture, the one darkness allowed Gina to escape witnessing, was no more appetizing: Sixty-four AK-47 slugs riddled the chief and his wife.

"Hurry up, Gina. We've got to get the hell out of here," Teresio bellowed. The pair scampered out of the dead police chief's home, but on their way out, Teresio took care to deposit a placard proclaiming the SMF's responsibility for the murders. It was scrawled with Albanese's blood, and Teresio was almost giddy with the boldness of this stroke and with excitement over this new SMF triumph. Gina concentrated only on stifling the riotous queasiness in her stomach.

Gina's route into the SMF may have been a twisted, confusing mélange of cul-de-sacs and faltering steps. Not so for Teresio's. His evolution into a murdering Maoist was straightforward business. Teresio's youth had as its hallmark poverty. His parents did not so much mistreat him as ignore him. But school provided the boy a release and, at age eighteen, his dedication to learning paid off with a scholarship to study economics at the University of Turin. Again, he plunged into his studies, but in short order, as he explained later to Gina, he found that his thinking led directly to the "inexorable logic of Marx's dialectic." The transition came abruptly. It took just a peek into Marx's seminal *Das Kapital* and Teresio had—he just knew—stumbled upon the solution to the injustices and miseries that had plagued his life. Teresio speedily pruned his personal reading list of the texts assigned by his professors and substituted a heavy diet of leftist tracts.

Not unexpectedly, his grades plummeted, and when he failed to win an appointment to a teaching fellowship, Teresio saw but one career open to him: full-time revolutionary. He dropped out of the university and never looked back on his career choice. He had no reason to. Teresio bubbled with a hatred for the rich, a hatred that could be satisfied only by the elimination of all of Italy's wealthy.

Revolution, that's what Teresio craved. A revolution to reverse economic injustices was, in his mind, the *only* solution. Mao, the most recent architect of a successful revolution, vaulted to the top of his heroes list, and Teresio increasingly saw himself as Italy's Mao. Certainly, he conceded, revolution would bring pain. And a quotation from Mao justified whatever violence and pain were necessary to do the job: "Everything reactionary is the same; if you don't hit it, it will never fall." Teresio was eager to do the hitting; he *wanted* to see lines of pain etched deeply into the faces of the rich.

That, at least, was Teresio's starting point. But over the years, his revolutionary fervor had dimmed, he began to question the feasibility of revolution. Italy's poor had been handed chance after chance to strike mortal blows against the wealthy classes, yet they turned down the opportunity again and again. Teresio admitted he could not understand it, but the poor in Italy did not share his overriding hatred of the rich.

Fuck 'em all, Teresio had finally decided, although that was a decision he kept even from Gina. Revolution might be a child's fantasy, Teresio's new thinking went, but hatred was not. It was hatred that he would nurture, and hatred was the weapon he intended to turn against the rich to achieve his own ends.

There was no joking, no bluff in Teresio. Not now. The hundreds, rich and poor alike, who had happened to be in the Turin Post Office when the bomb exploded now stood as monuments to the deadly earnestness of Teresio's scheming. So did the corpses of Dalla and Signora Albanese. Teresio, as Turin was sorrowfully learning, was in no mood to jest.

No laughing was overheard in Stone Williams's New York apartment either. Work was proceeding slowly on Anti-Terrorist, an electronic game Stone had begun designing in the aftermath of the first wave of horrors in Turin. Early in his career as a "tactical advisor," the ambiguous term Stone preferred to describe his S-COM exploits, he decided to invent a cover, and electronics game designer was it. It was a typically neat solution. Stone was already spending thousands of dollars yearly on every television and computer game that came along. S-COM assignments flowed in steadily, but the gaps between jobs maddened the workaholic in Stone. Games provided a valued release; he loved the orderly flow of battle that games provided and that real life never did.

Better still, with his cover in place, Stone began to invent his own games, designed to be more challenging than the conventional fare that glutted the marketplace. But even he was surprised when his early games proved popular and major manufacturers began to put in hefty bids for marketing rights. Stone's was a cover that turned a profit, and better than that there is not.

The cake came with icing, too. Stone's cover shielded him from prying Federal eyes interested in making an arrest under the U.S. Neutrality Act. That hoary statute forbids U.S. citizens from engaging privately in warfare on behalf of foreign countries, and it was a law that Stone and his S-COM comrades habitually broke. Stone knew well that successful prosecutions under that vague law were as rare as honesty is among narcotics cops, but his zeal for privacy made even the remote possibility of arrest unappetizing. Solid covers, like Stone's, afford a dollop or three of safety against gung-ho prosecutors on the make for sensational cases, and if the details of Stone's S-COM career ever surfaced publicly, even in expurgated form, it would be one hell of a sensation.

Today, however, Stone's thoughts were miles removed from covers, laws, and S-COM, too. The damn Anti-Terrorist game just wasn't meshing, he knew angrily. He knew why too. No matter how he attempted to set up the police anti-terrorist force—and he had tried every parameter—every gambit employed by the police departments he was acutely familiar with, the terrorists won. Each time. A dedicated terrorist, Stone found himself concluding, may die in the process, but precisely because his own death is not viewed as a barrier, that terrorist will whip you. He will blow up buildings with impunity, from the University of Wisconsin Mathematics Complex and the Mobil Oil offices through the Turin Post Office. He will hijack airplanes, kidnap government officials and the rich, and sometimes commit murder. The police, Stone clearly saw as his game plan unfolded, could make arrests, but terrorism still persisted. And, Stone began to fear, it will continue to flourish, until the police forces charged with its control themselves adopt unorthodox responses. Treat a terrorist as an ordinary criminal, Stone saw more sharply as he fiddled with his designs, and you will never succeed. A politician gone amok, that's what a terrorist is. To whip him, the response must take into account his rational irrationality, his insane sanity. Paradoxical? Certainly. But a joy for Stone Williams and the vision that guided him in developing a series of game plans for use by police. Neutralize the terrorist's insanity, that's the first, the critical step. Treat him with respect, not contempt, and keep stretching out the time, because time inevitably works against the terrorist. Make him see that the longer he persists, the surer his death is. Get him to mull on that, *calmly*. As time erodes his defenses, the terrorist's will ebbs, and the odds that he will surrender mount.

Voilà, Stone applauded himself. But the applause was not fully convincing. While Stone remained confident that he could plug these variables into Anti-Terrorist, it was just a game. Reality could offer much different variables. It was never so orderly, Stone knew, as mathematically configurated game designs. In a game everything is decidable, there are no hazy areas, and by game's end the winner and loser are undisputed. Not so in life. Stone might have wished—and wished he assuredly did—that life itself was ruled by logical order. But it was not, despite Stone's best efforts to make it so. He would not give up trying; surrender was not Stone Williams's style.

But neither would he shut himself off blindly to the disorder of life.

The ringing of his phone snapped Stone's attention on Anti-Terrorist.

"Hey, man, who's the SMF?" Myles Benet, a sergeant under Stone in Nam and—Stone often thought—S-COM's most dependable clutch killer, filled Stone in on the reason for his question. "Couple of days ago they blew up the Turin Post Office, right? Now they've murdered Turins' police chief and his wife. Looks like there's a new power in terrorism, Stone."

"The police chief?" Myles's news did not shock Stone. It was almost predictable.

While Myles sketched the latest facts from Turin, Stone's mind drifted to another call from Myles, the one that prompted Stone to join his Army buddy in peddling weapons, from Ingram machine pistols through "late model, cherry-condition tanks," Myles guffawed. Myles, Stone remembered, smiling to himself. A Haitian-born, South Bronx-bred black teamed with a Philadelphia mainline scion. An odd couple. But Stone and Myles shared complete trust—and, where soldiers are concerned, few facts are more meaningful.

"Yep, Myles, the SMF is carving itself a reputation," Stone said when his thoughts came back to the present. "Trouble is, nobody knows anything about them. But stay tuned. They're edging toward a big score. I can smell it."

"From four thousand miles away?" Myles, who could never resist a joke, parried. "My, my, what a nose. You rich kids can really do it all." With that, their conversation degenerated into a few concluding moments of banter before Stone, ever conscious of the flow of time in a life he sensed would be too short, cut off their talk. Still, Myles never failed to make the stolid Stone—"Indeed, your parents called that one right," Myles ribbed him—double up in laughter. The release from tension was good. Inevitably, however, Stone hungered to return to business, and Myles, a self-taught but keenly perceptive psychologist, always knew when to give him that space. Just as he knew when to kid Stone.

CHAPTER 3

Maria DiGrazia stretched up to the extent of her five-feet two-inch height while reaching into the cupboard for sugar to sweeten the coffee she had made for her bodyguards. The men, Guido and Ray, appreciated her eagerness to make them comfortable on the job. Other clients often insisted they spend their entire eight-hour shift outside, rain or shine. But Maria smilingly welcomed them as guests in her father's home. That was a switch, one they liked. They liked even more the extended view of Maria's shapely body and the way her one-hundred and seven pounds made for an absorbingly feminine shape without a hint of fat. Top off her enticing body with a slimly delicate face, olive skin, and ocean-blue eyes, and what Guido and Ray saw in Maria was a dream. And that's about the only place either man could get to a romantic base with Maria—in their dreams. Not that Maria DiGrazia, the intelligent and desirable daughter of a wealthy man, viewed her guards snobbishly. No, Maria simply took to heart the wishes of her father and the dicta of her church. Hers was a body preserved for a husband, and at age twenty and still a student at the Galileo Ferraris National Electrotechnic Institute, Maria's dance card did not presently include a husband or even a fiancé. Marriage loomed several years down the road. For now, Maria assiduously pursued her engineering studies and waited for the day her education would prepare her to assume a job with Especiale at her father's side. His instinctive chauvinism showing, Salvatore DiGrazia had originally scoffed at her plans, but he denied Maria nothing. Both knew it, and her superlative record at Galileo Ferraris underlined her ability to handle top-rung automotive work. Her joining the firm was a day father and daughter happily looked forward to.

"Your coffee, gentlemen," Maria said as she carried a tray laden with steaming cups and creamy cannolis into the DiGrazia living room. "I hope you like it. My father roasts the coffee beans himself."

One short sip informed Guido and Ray that they had never tasted coffee this good. Nor had they had a client as unaffectedly endearing as Maria DiGrazia.

"Tell me, on your jobs, uh"—Maria searched for the properly innocuous phrasing—"have you ever had trouble?"

Ray and Guido, they acknowledged, had been working as partners for a few years. It was a good job, bodyguarding. The pay was high. But no, they had encountered no dangers, they somewhat ashamedly admitted.

"Ah, but you must be very good, then," Maria said to put them at ease. "Your presence alone scares off terrorists." The idea was not farfetched. Both men ranked as tall, especially among the comparatively short-of-stature Italian citizenry. Guido measured six feet; Ray, but a fraction shorter. Plenty of pasta, pastries, bread and butter pushed their weight close to two-hundred pounds apiece. Fat they were not, however. They sported deceptive pot bellies, but beneath the flab rippled copious layers of muscle made hard by the hours of construction work both had pursued before turning to the more lucrative profession of bodyguarding. They obviously were tough men. Their beefy presence alone assured most clients that all would be safe, and that brawn is why their security firm had hired them despite their lack of prior training or experience.

"I must be off now. To school," Maria said when Ray popped the last of his cannoli into his mouth. "I'll be back in a few hours. See you later."

Her ploy nearly succeeded. Both guards started to say their goodbyes. Then the light flashed. She was their charge, and under the contract inked by Mr. DiGrazia, solo trips for Maria were absolutely forbidden.

Maria smiled sweetly when her guards jumped to their feet and hastened after her amidst a flurry of apologies for having to intrude. She was not testing their competency, although Guido wondered if that was the point. Maria is as Maria is, and that is playful. Besides, she admitted to herself when her guards foiled her unaccompanied exit, this bodyguard business *is* a nuisance. Tête-à-têtes with would-be suitors were out. No man could be expected to brave the gantlet composed by her hulking guards. Nor was Maria herself thoroughly comfortable with their constant presence. But, if it made Papa happy . . . Maria resigned herself to day-and-night guards.

"I'll drive, Miss DiGrazia," Guido stated matter of factly as they neared her car, the specially built Especiale her father had presented Maria on her eighteenth birthday. Designed and furnished personally by papa, Maria's sleek turquoise Especiale, complete with white-leather bucket-seats and a Sicilian-wood dashboard, attracted gazes even in car crazy Turin, where customized Maseratis, Ferraris, and Lolas qualified as ordinary fare. Then again, it might be the driver, Maria, who won the attention. But now it was Guido who grabbed the wheel. Ray followed in a backup vehicle. They were getting down to business.

Maria resented that. Not their professionalism, but being deprived of driving her Especiale. She resented too the closed-circuit camera Salvatore DiGrazia had installed that very morning to record the doings on the driveway and at their home's front door. An ounce of prevention, he had explained. Maria could not quibble with that homily, and as she thought about it, she granted that her annoyance with the camera was petty. Even the presence of bodyguards in her classes would be okay. Nowadays, it seemed half the students already had guards anyway. All that was fine.

What was not fine, not at all, was Guido's driving. Maria, every inch her father's daughter, thrilled in the pulsating feel of the Especiale's powerful twelve-cylinder engine. A light touch on the gas and, varoom, everything seemed within reach. In compact Europe, it *was*. An Especiale hits 165 miles per hour without panting. That velocity came effortlessly. Handling an Especiale was a feast for the driver; one that Guido was enjoying while Maria went hungry. But, she sighed to herself, he does seem to be having fun. Indeed Guido was. A broad smile crossed his face the instant he had turned the ignition key and the Especiale's insistent exhaust note began its rumble. Maybe, Maria thought, I'll stay a passenger until the troubles blow by. It cannot last for long.

Had Maria asked Guido's views at that moment, his answer would have differed. With a pretty girl at his side and an Especiale to command, Guido wanted nothing more than for this assignment to last forever. It would not.

Salvatore DiGrazia relished Saturday night. Another long work week at Especiale ended and Saturday was the one night of the week his demanding schedule afforded ample time for a leisurely dinner. Tonight, as frequently happened, his dining companions were Maria and Sophia, the two women in his life. The only women, for DiGrazia had vowed at his dying wife's bedside never to make love to another woman. His second vow was to keep Maria well and happy no matter what. Those vows he kept; Salvatore DiGrazia kept every vow he made—except, he sheepishly admitted, his annual New Year's resolution to forgo smoking. A good meal, in DiGrazia's judgment, was incomplete without the finishing touch of espresso and a cigar. And that's exactly what he looked forward to: a good meal, strong espresso, and a good cigar. Then Sunday would arrive and, with it, an afternoon of unmarred peace. DiGrazia counted himself a blessed man.

Mario DelRay, too, looked forward to Saturday nights. This one was particularly welcome. The successor to the deceased Dalla Albanese in the police chief's job, DelRay found that his life had been transformed into an endless web of bitter press conferences. At each one, reporters pointedly interrogated DelRay on when the terrorist siege of Turin would stop. Will there be arrests soon in the post office case? What about the Albanese murders? Do you have solid clues? DelRay, a smooth bureaucrat whose climb to the pinnacle of the Turin Police Department hinged not upon successes in breaking big cases but on his easy-going personality, swore to the reporters that investigations were making "sizable progress" and arrests could be expected "within days." Air, not facts or reliable leads, backed up DelRay's promises. The Seventh Mao Force left no clues, just bodies. Even the blood-scrawled note that bragged of the SMF responsibility for the Albanese killings failed to yield a single usable fingerprint.

Slick, this SMF is damned slick, DelRay thought. They made no mistakes, and until they do, Turin is theirs. But Saturday night and Sunday are mine. Maybe, come Monday, there'll be a break in the case, DelRay hoped against hope.

Saturday nights in the lives of Vincent Teresio and Gina Frugis never proved special. Only more of the same: more cheap food, "and if we're lucky, a bottle of bad wine," Teresio cursed. DelRay's reflections, if Teresio had known them, would have cheered him. Slick indeed. Teresio would have been proud. But no compliments derailed his coalescing plans, and he had reserved tonight for sketching the third prong of his unfolding scenario to Gina.

"Gina, what would you do with a million bucks?"

"Get serious, Vincent. A million? Right now I'd settle for ten dollars. At least we'd have food for a few more days."

"I *am* serious, Gina."

Gina immediately recognized Teresio's tone. Humor him; it was the only way.

"You know what I'd do. Use the money to help preserve our art, Italy's heritage."

"You would keep nothing for yourself?" Teresio pried.

"Sure. Some. Enough to live on."

"What if you could have lots to live on plus lots more to save as much art as you liked."

"That, Vincent, would be heaven. Not earth."

"Nope, Gina. Not according to my plan. The way I see it, a week from today we'll be sitting in a shitpot more than one million. Enough to save your art, give a few bucks to Turin's poor, buy Balducci's and make it into a soup kitchen *and* have plenty left over to set us up in houses, cars, and, what the fuck, boats even. For life."

"A dream, Vin. Not a very Maoist one at that."

"Mao, schmao, Gina. We've done our bit for the revolution. We've sacrificed for years. *Nobody* has done more. But there ain't no revolution. I'm not saying we'll be capitalist pigs. Hell no. We'll be rich revolutionaries, that's what. Sure it sounds contradictory, but I know *we* can do it. We can try, can't we?"

Gina knew better than to press her irrefutable point. Teresio's vision was contradictory, she knew. She knew as well that she also would like a more comfortable life. A few dresses, a bed with sheets, a home with heating. That all sounded irresistibly good.

Teresio's insistent voice awakened her to his sketch of the next step. "It will be our last, Gina. No more will be necessary. Think about this: Who has the money in Turin? The automobile families, that's who. They've parted with cash before when one of their own is kidnapped. Millions of bucks I'm talking about. They will do it again."

"They are not dumb, Vincent," Gina objected. "Even the third cousins of the Fiat and Ferrari owners employ armies of security men. It's not like boosting a bottle of champagne from Balducci's."

"Don't you be dumb, Gina. I know all that. But I've been doing research. Can't let those years of economics study go to waste, you know. Scratch the big two in cars and you've scratched the surface, that's all. Ever hear of Especiale?"

Yes, Gina had seen the luxurious cars that wear the Especiale marque, and more than once she had envied the exquisite sense of artistic creation that seemed to guide the maker of those elegantly powerful machines.

"The artist, as you would call him," Teresio impatiently elaborated his plan, "is Salvatore DiGrazia. He owns Especiale, lock, stock, and gearshift. It's a privately held corporation; there are no co-owners, zero partners. DiGrazia is it. Mull on this, Gina: Each Especiale that rolls off the assembly line wears a price tag above forty-thousand dollars. Whenever the cash register rings, DiGrazia shoves, what, five grand in his personal pockets. Sell two hundred Especiales a year and that's a million bucks. In profits. But DiGrazia don't sell no two hundred Especiales yearly; it's more like twenty thousand. Meaning he's socking away one-hundred million bucks every three hundred and sixty-five days."

"Christ, Vin, that's two million a week!" Gina, reeling in the face of that awesome mathematics, gasped.

"Exactly, kid. Exactly. DiGrazia's not as famous as Ferrari, but I'll bet you this: He's a fuck of a lot richer."

"With those bucks he must be guarded by a private army," Gina predicted.

"Nope. Not a single guard. I checked him out a coupla weeks ago. Cased his villa. Applied for a job at Especiale so I could look it over. Ha! They hired me too," Teresio gloated. " 'Course I didn't take their piddling offer. I've something a whole lot better-paying in mind: DiGrazia himself. There are no guards on him! Ever. He walks around free as a bird. What we're gonna do, Gina, is put that little bird in a cage and keep him there until the family buys his freedom. It's a piece of cake, and we'll be eating the icing for the next hundred years, Gina. We are going to be rich. That is a promise. Rich!"

"Promised Stone I'd be there at his place by eight o'clock," Rod Turnbull mumbled absently to himself as he reared away from a P.J. Clarke's bar stool. Rod, by all reckonings, figured as S-COM's quintessential soldier, and that was the *only* profession this son of Australia's barren outback ever aspired to. The whizz of fatally speeding bullets ironically pumped life into him. If he had not bumped into Stone Williams in Vietnam during a tour with Australia's army, this born non-com would have spent—or wasted, odds are—his life soldiering in Africa's deepest reaches as a mercenary for Rhodesia or South Africa. Fighting was the only life he knew, other than the hard-scrabble ranching he pursued as a boy with his father in Australia's deserts.

When Stone Williams entered Rod's life, his options broadened. So did his life span. Rod had caught a slug—

it was a nasty hole—in Nam. When Stone stumbled upon Rod's barely conscious form, he had lifted the bleeding Aussie to his shoulders and lugged him back—Cong guns still blazing in the village—safely to the medics. Rod would never forget that debt. A promise to Stone was a promise Rod had to keep, no questions asked. That was Rod's code.

Rod denied himself that one last drink before shoving off to see Stone. Boredom between actions ate at him more ravenously than it did the other S-COM battlers, perhaps because Rod alone lacked a cover occupation with which to fill his idle hours. Drinking and barroom brawls provided bouts of merriment. Combat afforded genuine relief. Maybe, Rod hoped as he hurried to make his meeting with Stone, just maybe he's called me in to announce a new S-COM contract. That happy thought propelled Rod faster on his way.

On his way, too, to Stone's that night was Lucky Guerrero, S-COM's fifth and last member. A demolitions expert—his skills learned in the pugnacious anti-Castro community that flourished in Miami and thrives on fantasies of Castro's overthrow—Lucky tossed his hat into S-COM's ring soon after defecting from OMEGA-7 and its cabal of counterrevolutionary plotters. The group had disgusted Lucky when it hired itself out to handle the hit of Chilean leftist Orlando Letelier in Washington, D.C. There were no politics involved in the murder; just cash. Lucky had no brief with Letelier's politics, but he had less brief with hypocrites, and that is what he thought OMEGA-7s membership consisted of. Not that Lucky had switched his ideological allegiances; he still burned hot with hatred of the Castro regime. But the 1961 Bay of Pigs campaign was the main chance, Lucky came to believe as he matured. The anti-Castro forces blew it. Period. Castro will remain in power until the people now living in Cuba toss him out, and the pipe dreams of OMEGA-7 and their ilk will not hasten that day one minute.

S-COM, by contrast, is reality, Lucky thought. There is no room in Stone Williams's platoon for the ideological bullshit that impotent plotters indulge in. Hypocrisy is absent, too. *Every* S-COM transaction is for cash—and there never were attempts to mask the fact that money, not politics, bought S-COM's allegiance. Lucky doted on that total business posture. He doted as well on the plentiful free time between S-COM jobs, time he used to live life to its fullest. Fine clothes, sensual salsa music, and a stream of beautiful women were staples in Lucky's life. And his S-COM paychecks insured a lavishly steady flow of all three.

Hope Stone's got a new mission for us, Lucky caught himself thinking. That fleeting thought surprised him. Lucky, of all the S-COM fighters, often approached new assignments with little enthusiasm. A lover is what he fancied himself, not a fighter. But Lucky sold himself short. He *always* came through. He had to. No S-COM member could do less, not with Stone exactingly overseeing every step of every operation. These days, however, Lucky actively itched for a new job. Boredom, that's what it was. It had been months since he rigged a bomb or fired a gun, and dammit, he had to concede, it was time to get back in business. Time, Lucky grinned, to make a little spending cash. He rang Stone's doorbell eagerly. Money, he hoped, lurked within.

"Gentlemen—" Stone called his meeting to order right after his two soldiers arrived "—this is just a checking-in, an inspection. There are no firm assignments on the books," Stone reported to the groans of Rod and Lucky alike. "But buck up, boys. I have a hunch that will soon change. Meantime, I have plenty of good Scotch, fine rum, and, yep, Rod, Foster's beer direct from your homeland. Grill some steaks on the patio. Exchange reports. At ease in other words. At fucking ease," Stone—eyeing Rod's habitual nervous finger tapping—barked.

Much as he respected Stone, Rod never felt at ease with him—except in battle, where the differences in their backgrounds and educations were erased by the roar of exploding cartridges. Easy-going Lucky, on the other hand, felt relaxed everywhere—even when he was deactivating a bomb that could level the entirety of New York's Midtown. And with their "Latin lover"—as S-COM called Lucky—leading the way, the three plunged into booze and recollections of the multi-million-dollar weapons sale to OMEGA-7 that had firmed the ties that made S-COM possible.

Lucky had found himself smack on the verge of bailing out of OMEGA-7. But to smooth his departure he agreed to handle one last gig: Serving as go-between in a massive purchase of automatic rifles, mortar, and heavier arms. What OMEGA-7 planned to do with these armaments he had not known, and had avoided asking. But a man named Stone Williams, he had heard, could produce the goods and would ask no questions if the cash was there. So Lucky made his pitch to Stone, and Stone, with Myles Benet and Rod in tow to afford the protection every gunrunner needs in the shadowy world of illegal weapons sales, came up with OMEGA-7's shopping list, a tank included. How Stone did it Lucky still did not know; Stone had his confidences, and Lucky respected them—then and now.

But for Lucky that snap of a deal proved to be a piece of luck indeed. He had lived up to his name once again. Stone found the straight-dealing Cuban to his liking and that he was an explosives expert with skills in small arms implanted Lucky's name deep in Stone's memory. When S-COM fell into place, Stone cautiously opted to include a "burn and blow boy." Lucky got the call, one he happily accepted. He had never regretted his choice. Nor had Stone.

With the food and drink, plenty of both, in their bellies and the reminiscent conversation dwindling to a halt, Stone reluctantly called a close to the evening's festivities. Meetings with S-COM fighters were a pleasure Stone rarely enjoyed, except when business called them together. He did not like taking the chance. S-COM made enemies by the bushel during every operation, and these enemies, most of them at any rate, dealt in death. S-COMers in a group made a tempting target, Stone calculated, and he did not wish to offer *any* temptation to would-be assassins. But tonight the chance had to be taken. Every intuition that Stone had telegraphed a single message: S-COM would soon be in action. His frequent telephone conversations with Leah and Myles clued him in to where they stood: They both hungered for action. But since he rarely had contact with Lucky or Rod, his precise commander's intellect wanted a fresh look. That night's party confirmed their readiness in Stone's mind. And if the exacting Stone Williams awarded them high grades, they were ready.

CHAPTER 4

"Sure, boss. I'll work today," Guido greeted the owner of the security agency when his telephone rang early that Sunday morning. Ray chimed in his availability as well. They both knew that the spread of terrorism throughout Italy had vaulted the demand for guards skyward. Six-day work weeks proved the rule, and this week it would be seven. They were tired; the mounting workload gave them scant time for relaxation. But the pay was good and Sunday duty tours and double-time salaries bloated their pay checks. Besides, guarding Maria DiGrazia was the best job they had had. Both looked forward to afternoon sips of the DiGrazia special coffee, and what the hell, it was Sunday—they'd sweeten the brew with anisette. The job could be fun, and for sure, *nothing* happens in Turin on Sundays.

"Maria, you look delightful today. As usual," Salvatore DiGrazia complimented his daughter when she entered the dining room to eat her standard breakfast: a tumbler of orange juice and a single slice of buttered toast.

"I must watch my figure, Papa," Maria answered her father's daily complaint about her lack of enthusiasm for food. But Papa had a ready retort: "Worry not, Maria. *Everybody* watches your figure," he chuckled proudly. DiGrazia knew that, misplaced as parental pride often is, his was superbly justified.

"Are you working today, Papa," Maria asked between tiny bites of toast.

"You forget, Maria. Today is Sunday. I thought you'd like to go on a picnic. A slow drive into the country. A basketful of cheeses, good Genoa salami, bread, some Chianti. It'll take us away from Turin, from the agonies of the last week."

Maria never refused her father. This time would be no exception. Whenever the weather turned nice, Salvatore DiGrazia hankered for a Sunday picnic. It reminded him, he told Maria, of the picnics he and her mother had enjoyed during their courtship. DiGrazia had had little money in those days, when Especiale was but a garage he rented and in which he serviced the cars of friends and stole moments to tinker with a prototype vehicle he insisted to doubters—and there were many—would revolutionize the world of car making. Broke or not, however, DiGrazia always managed to scrape together a handful of lira to buy a jug of wine and fresh bread, and those inexpensive outings with Maria's mother-to-be fired his resolve to make Especiale a name to be reckoned with. Make no mistake, DiGrazia did not crave money for himself. He lived a simple life even when times were fat at Especiale. But for his wife and the bustlingly large family he envisioned, DiGrazia wanted only the best. The self-made man, there is no denying, had made Especiale a household name for automotive excellence. But that was afterwards—after his wife's death in childbirth. That had slowed him; for months he brokenheartedly brooded over her loss. But as he watched the bubbly baby Maria grow, DiGrazia's enthusiasm was rekindled. He had new causes to battle for, Maria ranking very high among them. The loss of Maria, DiGrazia knew, would be too much to bear, and that's precisely why guards now shadowed her every step.

Salvatore DiGrazia consequently smiled with relief when Maria's day-shift guards arrived. Another ounce of protection was in place, one that would make the picnic more carefree. The firm the guards represented came with the highest recommendations. The best in Turin, he had been assured. With them around, there's nothing to fear, claimed his business associates.

Still, DiGrazia could not help but be a bit fearful and protective where Maria was concerned. But the barely visible bulges he detected under the armpits of the guards reassured him. They came prepared. That was good. Now it was time to prepare for their picnic, a task DiGrazia reserved for himself, just as he had in those earlier days with Maria's mother. This time it would take a mite longer. Guards, DiGrazia figured, get hungry too. Food for four, not two, was the order of the day.

"Jesus, Vin! Don't flash the gun like it's a toy," Gina Frugis hissed as Teresio playfully pulled his AK-47 out of its sack for a final look.

"Worrywart. Remember Mao's saying: 'We need an enthusiastic but calm attitude.' What's the big deal? Nobody's looking," Teresio said and shrugged off her criticism. "It's Sunday morning, for chrissake. Everybody's at church or sleeping off last night's vino. Hell, Gina, if anybody saw this baby"—Teresio merrily displayed the brutish weapon on the deserted Turin street where they walked—"all they'd do is run. *Nobody* is gonna argue with this machine. Nobody who wants to live."

Gina conceded there were no witnesses to Teresio's brazen gun toting. Even so, the awkwardness of parading down a public street carrying illegal weapons in broad daylight gnawed at her. But they lacked a car, and as Teresio pointed out, they would be even more conspicuous on a bus. "Better to walk the two miles," he had argued, and lacking a better plan, Gina had offered no resistance. What they would do once they kidnapped DiGrazia was another matter, an open question neither had thought to close. The exhiliration Teresio felt over the prospective snatch made him even less methodical and careful than usual.

Nor was Gina in a mood to wrestle with the intricacies of the operation. The thought of this kidnapping made her uneasy, and Teresio's budding capitalism confused her. But this was no time for Gina Frugis to analyze details, for even the broader picture confused her. But as she always did, she would go along with Teresio. Shit, she kicked herself, it has come to the point where we're married. Married to each other and to the SMF. Divorces are complicated when murders clutter the past, and irked as it made her feel, Gina found herself slipping into the traditional, unquestioning role of the Italian wife. That was the shocker. Gina Frugis: liberated woman, art student. Gina Frugis: wife. The equation boggled her mind. When this kidnapping ended, when they had pocketed the loot Teresio promised would be theirs, then she would allow herself time to probe that transformation. Try as she might, however, it continued to irritate her like a burr under a saddle. It just made no sense. Then again, not much in Gina's life made sense to her right now. These were just more befuddling elements in an absolutely bemusing jigsaw puzzle.

Neither puzzles nor Gina's rapt introspection concerned Teresio as the pair neared the DiGrazia villa. Money did, and the smell of ready cash seemed to Teresio to get more pungent the nearer they came to the DiGrazia address.

"See, Gina. No guards. Not even a fence," Teresio chuckled when they reached DiGrazia's home. "Put this on," he commanded as he handed Gina a ski mask. "If any witnesses live, they'll be worthless to the police—"

"Because," Gina joked to relieve her of her tensions, "they'll say skiers did it."

"This, Gina, is not a comedy."

"Fuck you, Vin."

The opening of DiGrazia's front door halted their squabble.

"Who's that, Vincent?"

"Beats the shit out of me," Teresio admitted. "Must be DiGrazia's girlfriend. Maybe his daughter."

Teresio got it right the second time. Maria, meantime, busied herself checking the tire pressures on her Especiale in anticipation of the Sunday drive with Papa. She again made it out of the house a few paces ahead of Guido and Ray, who—when they noticed the disappearance of their charge—rushed out, too.

Occupied with her car, Maria failed to observe the strange masked pair lurking at the end of the driveway. They were partially shielded by bushes, but Guido alertly made up for Maria's omission. "Excuse me, sir"—can't be rude in these rich neighborhoods, Guido reminded himself. It could cost a man his job and for all Guido knew the masked duo could be friends of the family with a zest for pranks—"have you an appointment with Mr. DiGrazia?"

Ray fingered his gun anxiously while they waited for an answer.

Teresio's response came louder than expected. More deadly, too. His snorting AK-47 did all his talking, and before Gina withdrew her gun from its sack, Guido and Ray lay in pools of their own blood. A spray of bullets had almost severed Ray in two; his stomach lay ripped open for inspection of that morning's scrambled eggs and sausage. Guido got a better shake: Just three bullets tore into his head. But he was every bit as dead.

Gina's vomit came up fast. With no breakfast in her belly, it was pure bile. But its upward rush could not be stopped. The sight of the mangled, bleeding corpses stood ineradicably in her eyes. She sprayed the DiGrazia driveway with her vomit.

"In the car, bitch," she heard. But Teresio's shouted order was directed not at her but at the woman by the car. "You, too, Gina. In! Hurry!"

Gina followed blindly. She felt too bad to argue, and sick or not, she knew this was not the time.

"Drive! Fast!" Teresio leveled the gun barrel at Maria's stunned face. Her options were nil. She cranked the car, feathered the accelerator, and for the first time in their lives, Gina Frugis and Vincent Teresio found themselves chauffered passengers in a luxury Especiale.

Do what he says, Maria repeated to herself. Don't argue. He's nuts. Obviously. A killer. Every instinct she had begged her to submit—except for her heart which beat away its insistent demand that she do something. But Maria wisely ignored her heart. Thank God Papa was inside, Maria realized. Thank God.

Fortunately for Maria, no move against Teresio was possible. Not in the snug confines of an Especiale with an AK-47 pointed at her head. The man, she sensed as her brain firmly took control over her heart, is a killer. A mindless thug. With that picture painted, however, Maria could make no plans. All she could do was exactly what Teresio ordered, and right now that was, "Go faster, cunt. Faster!" Teresio shrieked in his anxiety.

Gina wanted just two things: a drink of water to cleanse the foul taste out of her mouth and to be free of the ludicrously tight confines of the Especiale. Great cars Especiales might be, but for two, not three. If Teresio pulls the trigger, the recoil would surely knock my teeth out, Gina speculated as she rolled down the passenger-side window and jammed her head into the refreshing air.

Teresio sat on Gina's lap and struggled to keep balance as he maintained a steady aim at Maria's head. He had to admire her driving skills. Each of his barked directions was smoothly executed, even though their speed rested at 65 miles per hour and—in his agitation—Teresio gave his commands to turn right, turn left with no warning. Maria nonetheless made the demanded turns on dimes, and Teresio contentedly knew that no stodgy police car could keep pace. Not that he seriously feared one was following. This *is* Turin, he knew, and hours would click by before the police picked up the trail. And by then Teresio figured to know who he had snatched and what the price tag would be. Fuck the police, Teresio sneered; they would be no problem at all. Not with the SMF in the homestretch.

"They kidnapped my daughter," Salvatore DiGrazia wept inconsolably into his telephone.

"Calm down, Mr. DiGrazia," Police Chief DelRay soothed. It took effort on DelRay's part. This Sunday morning interruption irked him. The goddamn rich, he thought between the unctuous homilies he offered DiGrazia, think they can disturb anyone's peace. True enough, DiGrazia had apologized for calling, but when he burst into his report of murdered bodyguards and a snatched daughter, DelRay instantly recognized trouble. DiGrazia, DelRay's memory told him, did not rank among Turin's very wealthiest, but the man had money, influence, and popularity enough to make an enormously unpleasant stir.

"Something *must* be done. Now, Chief." DiGrazia's voice begged for more than the empty phrases that the chief had been uttering.

"I promise you, Mr. DiGrazia. A dozen men will be on the job within a half-hour. We'll have your daughter back safe and sound by nightfall—at the latest."

When DiGrazia hung up, he already knew the Turin police could accomplish nothing. DelRay's nonchalance clinched it. This did not surprise DiGrazia; he had placed the call because there was no other place to turn. The bodyguards were dead. He had known that before seeing the massacre on the driveway. The shots that had echoed in the kitchen were not pistol fire. No handgun made that incessant chatter. That Maria was missing was a relief of sorts—at least she had not died in the shoot-out. What the future held for Maria was another matter. DiGrazia could hazard no guess; he simply did not know. But he knew definitely that this case required far more than the Turin police force; experts had to be summoned. Price was no issue, not for DiGrazia. The world's best anti-terrorist team, that's what DiGrazia wanted. But who knew what that was? DiGrazia angrily admitted he had no idea. He knew only the Turin Police Chief.

"Up the stairs," Teresio snarled at Maria when they arrived at his home. "Gina, take her in and guard her. I'll ditch the car."

Maria obeyed this order, too. Calmer now, Gina silently showed Maria the way in as Teresio sped off in the Especiale. Once inside, Maria surveyed her surroundings:

The place appalled her. It stank of poverty, and Maria nearly found herself sympathizing with her abductors. Nearly, but not quite. The brutal slaying of her guards could not be forgotten. These people, Maria reminded herself, are killers—murderers who won't show me any pity. But the woman seems almost nice, Maria reflected. A pretty girl. Quiet. How did she get entangled in this insanity? Maria determined to find out. But for now she would ask no questions—not until the grim situation she found herself in cleared up.

"Sit there," Gina beckoned to the mattress, Teresio's only "chair." With an element of amusement, both women realized that Gina was playing hostess to Maria as guest. That sat fine with Gina. She told herself that harming this young woman fell far astray from her list of personal objectives. Gina had seen too much death already; the Albaneses and the vividly crimson corpses of the two dead guards tormented her mind's eye. She did not want to see more bodies, that she was sure of.

"How do you feel," Gina prodded herself to ask politely.

"Scared," Maria confessed. "Terrified. What happens now?"

Indeed, what does happen? Gina asked herself. Snatching DiGrazia himself might have made sense to Gina. But this girl? Will Teresio kill this kidnap victim, whether or not the ransom is paid? Ha, Gina's thoughts laughed. Maybe we'll convert her and she'll join the SMF, like that rich American girl who became a member of the Symbionese Liberation Army in California. That was the greatest laugh of all, one that improved Gina's mood. "Just be quiet. Don't fuck up," Gina advised with fantasies of Patty Hearst in her mind. "You'll come out of this all right."

Were Gina's words a promise? Or a prediction that could be grotesquely mistaken? Neither woman knew.

"A real pisser, that car is," Teresio bellowed as he entered the room. "Faster than a capitalist on his way to screw the poor. Damn thing does seventy miles per hour.

In first gear." Even though Teresio recognized that the car counted as the best lead police had in this case, he had prolonged his ride in it. The power he sensed while grasping the wheel and pressing the accelerator rivaled the sensations of squeezing the trigger of an automatic. A fleet of Especiales—Teresio would have a whole fleet, he decided. A car for each day of the week—and his take from this kidnapping would cover that cost with millions left over.

"Okay, woman. What's your name," Teresio got down to business.

The question stunned Maria. She had been kidnapped by people who did not even know who she was. Should she tell the truth? Or lie?

Teresio's sharp slap across her face solved that dilemma. "Answer me, bitch!"

"I am Maria DiGrazia. The daughter of Salvatore DiGrazia," she answered simply. Tell the truth, that's what the slap communicated to Maria. Tell a lie—say, maybe, that I am an Especiale secretary—and this lunatic will kill me. Just to dispose of unwanted baggage. He killed two guards; another corpse could make no difference to him.

"Whore! You're DiGrazia's mistress," Teresio announced. "The old cat has himself some young pussy." That had to be the explanation, Teresio guessed. DiGrazia, he remembered from an old newspaper article, was not married. A daughter? There would be none—at least none the old man owned up to.

Teresio's slander stung Maria. "You are mistaken. I am his daughter," she retorted firmly.

"Lies, bitch, make you dead," Teresio leered. "Keep shoveling that shit and—" he fingered a rusty Swiss army knife—"and I'll cut off your right tit." Those shapely globes captivated Teresio. DiGrazia could pick them, he conceded. The man had taste in cars and broads both.

"I am not lying; I'm sorry. . . ." The tears finally burst through Maria's stoic mask.

"That, cunt, costs you a tit." Teresio brusquely tore

open her blouse. The buttons popped to the floor as Maria, immobilized by fright, sobbed. Knife in hand, he moved to cut the bra strap that stood between Maria's breasts and his roaming fingers.

"Stop it, Vincent!" Gina interrupted. "This is getting us nowhere. Give her time to think. She will tell the truth once she knows exactly where she stands. This shit"—Gina angrily gestured at Teresio's knife—"will just scare her into telling more lies. We'll tie her up, put her in a closet, and let a couple of hours pass. She'll be ready to talk then."

Teresio surrendered reluctantly to Gina's suggestion. She was right, he agreed. But he could not take his mind off Maria's breasts as he began to bind her hands and feet. Like a schoolboy, he took every opportunity to graze his fingers against Maria's full bra cups. The sensations gave him an erection, one he vowed "this bitch will suck off" before he finished with her. Gina, Teresio thought to himself, could go finger herself for all he cared; what he wanted was a taste of Maria DiGrazia.

Thank you, Maria's eyes said silently to Gina. She had not known what this maniac might do to her. Whatever he had in mind, it would be awful, she was sure. Thank God for the woman, Maria thought. She might be a terrorist, but at least she is not a psycho like this Vincent.

The clicking of the teletype machine dragged Leah Aviv over to inspect the latest news bulletin. Another Sunday spent in the office, Leah shrugged as she marched from her desk to the persistent machine. The high-pitched, fast-paced demands of international public relations alone put thousands in their graves before their fortieth birthday rolled around to greet them. But Leah energetically held down an executive-level PR consulting post along with her connection to S-COM. It was a busy and full life, but Leah thrived on it. Besides, her overflowing schedule allowed no time for mournful rehashes of her husband's death in an ill-conceived and bungled Israeli Army covert operation in turbulent Lebanon. She had warned against that "op", and every confidential report gathered by Israel's Secret Service had indicated the impossibility of the proposed mission. It was a stupid, suicidal plan that was to mean only sure death for those sent to execute it. Bad enough that the Army decided to plow ahead with it anyway; much worse when David was ordered to participate. Leah howled when the colonel arrived at her doorstep to mournfully announce David's "honorable death in action." Honorable like hell, Leah protested—and kept up her attacks against high-level incompetence and its willful disregard for intelligence assessments until her superiors, feeling the strong pressures from above, reluctantly sacked this immensely skilled agent.

It was at David's funeral that Leah renewed her friendship with Stone Williams. She had known him well, even dated him a few times, when all three of them—Stone, David, and Leah—were Yalies. Stone had come to pay his last respects to his best friend, but before he departed Tel Aviv he had recruited a new member of S-COM: Leah. Her background in intelligence work was unsurpassed; her fluency in English, Russian, German, Hungarian, Hebrew, and Arabic put her at ease in diplomatic and espionage circles across the globe; and, although Stone but barely acknowledged this last reason even to himself, he was powerfully attracted to this gorgeous, black-haired daughter of Hungarian parents.

When Stone finally decided to offer Leah the chance to become S-COM's fifth member, she jumped at it. She had had her fill of bureaucratic espionage. Free-lance missions, S-COM style, provided far better opportunities for achieving Leah's personal goals, and high among them was the elimination of the terrorism that caused thousands of useless deaths throughout the steaming Mediterranean world.

"Not more terrorism," Leah said as she ripped the story off the clattering teletype. TURIN HEIRESS KIDNAPPED, the headline proclaimed. Digging into the facts presented by the wire service, Leah recognized the name

DiGrazia. During her stint with Israeli intelligence, she had worked closely with Salvatore DiGrazia several times. He had unquestioningly provided Leah with high-speed automobiles when delicate situations arose and Leah remained grateful to this man who demanded no assurances except that his cars would not be involved in murders. Exactly the opposite, Leah had explained, and DiGrazia—sensing that no fuller explanation would or could be offered without endangering lives—took her word at face value. Nor had Leah ever been forced to lie to him; and for that she was thankful. Lies and governmental espionage, she ruefully remembered, are inseparable—another reason she was overjoyed to be in the more straightforward world of S-COM.

But what, Leah mulled, could S-COM do to repay those old debts to DiGrazia? What, to get more to the point, could *she* do?

"We've fucked up, Vin. We didn't nab DiGrazia; we got this woman instead. Now what," Gina implored as her confusion exploded to the surface.

"Simple. We did *not* fuck up. Nope. We call DiGrazia —*after* we find out who the girl really is. Put a price on her head and DiGrazia pays it. There's no doubt. Capitalists like DiGrazia deal in buying and selling people. He'll come through. No way he's going to toss that fine snatch to the sharks. Only question is, how much is she worth? Dunno if we can get more than a million for a mistress, even a hot one like this girl."

"What if she really is his daughter, Vincent?"

"Come on! That is *nobody's* daughter. But," Teresio pondered the point, "if she is, that's so much the better. For us. The price goes up, Gina, way up."

While this prelude to bartering played itself out, Maria made do as best she could in the cramped, stuffy closet. The solitude was an improvement; at least she was removed from the stare and probing paws of "the nut." Her best bet, Maria increasingly saw, remained to be straight with her abductors, not provoke the man, and pray—

harder than she had ever before prayed in her life—that somehow Papa could win her freedom. Locked tight and bound in this dark closet, Maria knew that matters—especially where escape is concerned—had been removed from her hands. She could bide for time. That was all, she decided.

"Celebration time, Gina. Let's party," Teresio said jubilantly after he took a pair of marijuana joints from one of the many holes in the walls that surrounded them.

"Grass, Vincent? Where did you get it?"

"Two years, Gina. Two long years I've been waiting for the moment to fire up this reefer. Tonight's it. Five days from now, no more, we will be rich. Hell, Especiales in the driveway; reefer by the kilo; champagne by the Jeroboam; a house with plumbing," Teresio observed sardonically on his way to urinate out a crack in a boarded-up window. "Damn, Gina, it will be good, that's for fucking-a sure."

"But what about the revolution? What about Mao? Italy's deteriorating art? Everything we've fought for?" The list of palpable priorities jumbled through Gina's grass-clouded skull.

"What about them? We can have both, Gina. Money and revolutionary fervor. Just watch."

The contradictions, despite Teresio's blithely repeated assurances, did not resolve themselves in Gina's mind. Something was afoot here, but, Gina shrugged, it made zero sense. The killings of the past days. Now a kidnapping. And Teresio's enthusiasm for cars, money, drugs, booze, and the fineries of the wealthy. All were new. Gina wondered how the pieces fit together.

Teresio wondered not at all. The rush of events, not analytically decisive reasoning, catapulted him forward. It was main-chance time, he calculated. Grab the cash and run like hell. His escalating grass high, the sensations of unconscious weightlessness that grass always produced in him, prevented more probing analyses. Physical probing it did not prevent.

"Hmm. Let's screw, Gina." Teresio's hand moved in expanding circles up her back, and his fingers waited their turn to move in on Gina's breasts.

"Not now, Vincent. I'm thinking," Gina said absently, rebuffing his advances. Her mind kept trying to zero in on the glue that held the events of the past week together.

"Yum." Teresio mouthed her neck. "Think later; fuck now."

But try as he did—and that was hard—Teresio could not arouse Gina's interest in sex. "Goddamn bitch," he spat and rolled away from her. When Gina failed to notice his departure, that piqued him more, and her indifference made his erection throb harder.

"More than one way to skin a pussy," Teresio grumbled as he stalked over to Maria's closet and undid the hasp lock that kept her tightly within. "Out!," he ordered.

With her hands and feet securely bound, Maria nonetheless managed to crawl slowly toward her captor. But not quick enough: "Faster!" Teresio shouted, and a sharp boot to her ass punctuated the urgency of his command. "You rich bitches! Castrating cunts, that's what you are. But listen, girlie. Me, you are not going to castrate. Got it?"

A hard tug on her flowing hair prompted Maria to nod assent. What now, she fretted fearfully.

"Prove who you are," Teresio demanded as he untied the gag that silenced her. He left her hands and feet securely bound. "Show some ID."

Maria thought hard trying to come up with a way to satisfy her tormentor. But she had dropped her purse between the bodies of the dead guards. "I've nothing. It's all at home."

"Liar! You just don't want to show me." Teresio's eyes remained glued to her open blouse. He felt a twitch in his penis. "I'm gonna strip-search you," Teresio said. His hands seconded the motion by unfastening her bra. Without restraints, Maria's large breasts tumbled freely forward. In the rush of cool air, her nipples hardened and jutted out. Teresio's thumb pressed down on her right nipple; Maria instinctively tried to roll away from him, but Teresio's mind was made up. He could already see himself between Maria's generous but firm thighs. The image propelled him to begin undoing her skirt.

Gina's voice derailed his reverie. Her own thoughts about Teresio's unexplained personality switch plus her continuing unhappiness about this kidnap business at first had absorbed Gina's attention and prevented her from focusing on her partner's exploits. But now her attention fixed itself firmly on Teresio. Gina did not like what she saw. "Cut the shit, Vincent!"

"I'm gonna find out who this cunt is," Teresio threw back over his shoulder without bothering to take a look at Gina. He was too busy pulling down the zipper on Maria's skirt.

"Stop it or I'll kill you."

Teresio heard the ominous words. They made no sense. The voice did not belong to Maria; it was Gina who had spoken.

"Don't kid around, Gina," Teresio said as he tugged the unzipped skirt downward. Maria's pristinely white panties beckoned him onward.

"I'm not, Vincent." The warning words did not halt Teresio's progress. The unmistakable click of a clip being shoved into an AK-47 did. When he spun around, Gina's gun aimed directly at his chest.

"Ha, ha. This isn't funny, Gina." Teresio strained to sound calm. But no one *is* calm in the face of an automatic weapon. Teresio could hear his heart sending up a frantic beat.

"Neither is rape, Vincent. It's no joke. It is a bourgeois pig crime. Look in Mao's *Little Red Book*. Do the advancing Red Armies rape along their way? Bullshit, Vincent. That's what rape is. Pig bullshit." Gina unflinchingly pointed the AK-47 barrel at Teresio's midsection. He got the message.

"Rape, Gina? That's what you think? No, no. I was just going to strip-search her to see if she had hidden an ID card someplace weird. You know . . ." Teresio anxiously fumbled for an explanation that would soothe Gina.

"Yeah, I know. And you were going to probe inside her with your cock, right, Vincent? Just to make sure nothing was hidden?"

"You got it all wrong, Gina. I was searching her for *us.*"

Gina knew he was lying, but she could not bring herself to pull the trigger. She did not want more blood on her hands. Leave, she thought. Just stomp out. Forget the whole SMF jazz. That's what she wanted to do. But that would mean leaving the girl in his hands, and that Gina would not do. Not now.

"Okay, Vin. I misunderstood. But prisoners of war have rights, too. If anybody is going to search her body, I will do it. Right?" Gina indicated her peaceful intentions by slipping the clip out of her gun.

Teresio sighed with relief. He would get what he wanted from the girl *and* pay Gina back for this scare. But this, he perceived, was not the time. "Search her if you'd like, Gina. But on second thought, she didn't have time to hide anything."

Maria felt the murderous tension dissolving. She played her card. "You know, you could listen to a radio. The news will tell you who I am."

"Dumb cunt," Teresio roared. The endless stupidities they inflict on me, he thought. "Look around. See any lights in here? There's no electricity. You thought we burned candles for what? Atmosphere?"

Nor did he have a transistor radio, Maria guessed. No sense mentioning it and triggering another rage. But another light flashed in her brain. "The newspapers. They'll have a complete report."

"She's right, Vincent. Why don't you go out and see if this kidnapping rated a special edition or something?" Gina did not imagine there would be one, not on a somnolent Turin Sunday. But she welcomed an excuse for getting Teresio outside and away from her and the girl.

"Sure, Gina. No sweat." Teresio hoped the few minutes alone would give Gina time to calm down. What the hell, they might get lucky and the paper would solve the mystery of the girl's identity, Teresio figured. He whistled his way out of the room.

With Teresio gone, Gina turned to dressing Maria. A pull on the zipper and the skirt was back in place. But the blouse was hopeless. When Teresio ripped it, he tore most of the buttons off. Gina gently hooked Maria's bra—yes, she *did* have nice breasts, Gina noticed appraisingly. But the blouse would have to do as is. There was none to lend. Gina had only the Mona Lisa T-shirt that she wore.

"Thank you," Maria offered. She meant it. Gina, she knew, had saved her from getting raped. Maybe, Maria's mind whirred, maybe she'd let me go free. She just might, Maria hoped.

Before Maria could put that idea into motion, Teresio burst back in: "Hey, Gina! It is DiGrazia's daughter. *Il Messaggero* has a full page on us. A clockwork kidnapping, they said. The work of professionals! And, like she told us, she's Maria DiGrazia. Very big, very big bucks. DiGrazia's *only* child, it says here. . . . He's prepared to cooperate 'in full' with the kidnappers for the release of his daughter unharmed. Fat fucking city! How much do you think you're worth to your old man, whore?"

The question pained Maria. How much? How could she answer? How could this man so cavalierly put a price on someone's life? She managed to say noncommittally only that she had no idea.

"How much is he worth? What's he got in the bank?"

Maria spent the bulk of her free time poring over Especiale's production plans and accounting reports; she could unqualifiedly answer that question. To the nearest nickel. She chose, however, to mask her knowledge. It was none of this man's business, and, furthermore, Especiale and the DiGrazia family were far less wealthy than many supposed. The books proved it. Maria chose to tell Teresio none of this, although that, too, was a risk. What if he was disappointed by the sums her father could manage? It would be a pittance by Fiat standards, Maria knew. But even if she volunteered her insights, the man would disbelieve her. Probably try to beat her again. Better to play dumb—he would buy it, Maria figured. "I have no idea."

Teresio accepted that. Of course this "twat," which is all Teresio saw in Maria, she would know nothing about the family business. Sex, that's all she likely knew, and Teresio intended before finishing with her to find out exactly how much she knew about that.

"Let's put her back in the closet," Teresio commanded. He had resumed control of the operation. Gina let him have it. The deal made her increasingly ill. Teresio, on the contrary, felt overjoyed. "Fifty million bucks, easy. That's what I thought we'd get for DiGrazia. We didn't get him. But we got every bit as good. The girl is a gold mine; her father so much as promised to fork over the family jewels for her. We'll shoot for fifty mill, right, Gina?"

"Sure, Vincent." Gina could care less. It would not work. It had soured, the whole revolutionary bit had. That struck her when Teresio tried to rape Maria. They were bad revolutionaries, Gina sensed, and worse kidnappers. Hell, they had gotten the wrong target: the daughter and not the father. What a horrible start. The finish, Gina expected, would be more awful.

The mechanics of securing the ransom began to spring from Teresio's mouth. But his elaborate detail amounted to so much fanciful trivia in Gina's mind. She agreed to all without even listening. Her head nodded like a puppet's as Teresio made point after point.

Insincere as Gina's enthusiasm for Teresio's plan was, her ready consent pleased and satisfied him. She's okay, he reminded himself before drifting off into sleep. Still, he intended nonetheless to settle the score from this evening with her. But first came tomorrow and the countdown to riches. The future, Teresio gloated, looks tremendous.

Gina's sleep came more fitfully. More fitful, too, was her view of the future.

CHAPTER 5

"Another kidnapping in Italy," Stone muttered when Tom Brokaw recounted Sunday's events in Turin on the *Today* show. Stone, despite his penchant for electronics and like wizardry, despised television and especially loathed TV news. Television reportage amounted in Stone's mind to a surface skimming and, more often than not, a gross misunderstanding of the real news of the world—news that Stone kept abreast of by cultivating an army of intelligence community contacts. But he could not break the habit of gluing himself to the set for three doses of daily news. Even if the marionettes on channels 2, 4, and 7 could not tell a news lead from a "disinformation" plant, they nonetheless influenced and determined what millions of citizens less well-versed in the meaning of world events believed. So Stone steeled himself for his thrice daily bouts with the tube, and on rare occasions, this masochistic dedication paid off.

Today, Stone intuited, was one of those occasions. His ears tuned out Brokaw's drone to focus on Turin. He had been there once while making a roundabout delivery of Vietnam surplus M-16s to an anti-Qaddafi Libyan guerilla group. That had been a small-change run, just as the Libyan outfit turned out to be more small change that Muammer el-Qaddafi swiftly and brutally pocketed the instant they began to make annoying noises. But Stone had enjoyed those indirect glimpses of Qaddafi and his schemes for funding worldwide leftist revolutions—the Libyan leader was a man Stone wanted to tangle with, but, as always, Stone would wait for *his* time to arrive. For now, his thoughts centered on Turin and on the likely culprits behind the latest kidnapping: the Seventh Mao Force.

When Stone broke away from his still-meshing thoughts on the SMF to field a call on his private line, he immediately recognized the voice: "Stone, I'm worried about that girl in Turin. Maria DiGrazia," Leah confided. After Leah finished sketching her previous contacts with the DiGrazias, Stone shared her concern. But not unreservedly.

"S-COM," Stone reminded Leah, "is not the Red Cross." Charitable operations are out of the question when every S-COM mission puts the life of its members smack on the line, a line that frequently is no sturdier than a tightrope in a hurricane. "I track you one-hundred percent, Leah," Stone concluded. "But don't forget S-COM's one commandment: No backer, no fight. Missions of mercy make nice fantasies for romantic fools, but real-life 'ops' are our game."

Leah knew the rules. She had to concur with Stone: S-COM had to stay out of the Turin mess unless money was on the line. But Leah had to do *something* for DiGrazia; he had come through for her, and she could do no less for him.

Stone anticipated the train of Leah's thoughts. He knew her too well not to. "There is one thing we can do, Leah. You canvass your European intelligence sources on the SMF. I'll do the same here in the U.S. There's no doubt in my mind that the SMF is responsible, and perhaps we can leapfrog a step or two ahead of the police. Come up with concrete leads, and we'll pass them on to DiGrazia. Gratis."

Leah bought Stone's suggestion. Both recognized that it fell pitifully short of solving the problems that gripped DiGrazia and his daughter, but it was the best S-COM could offer.

"Keep in touch, Leah." Stone hung up and started to scout through his Rolodex for contacts to call.

"Stone!" The shout rang through his apartment. "Stone!"

"What's up, Penuche," Stone laughed. "Hungry?"

"Stone!" the gigantic palm cockatoo called again.

Stone hand-fed an orange slice to the yard-long, black, and plumed talking bird. Stone pampered his ten thousand-dollar Penuche. It was too precious a possession to ignore. Only one hundred palm cockatoos are found in the United States, and most reside in the close quarters of zoos, not the spacious splendor of an Eastside penthouse apartment—and Stone's bird had freedom of flight throughout the duplex.

Penuche's purchase, much as the orderly Stone might try to deny it, had been impulsive. It was, in fact, Stone's first frivolous act ever. He bought the bird the day his parents died in a puzzling private airplane crash. Penuche's funereal hue struck Stone as appropriate to the occasion, and just as importantly, he had reveled in the sheer impulsiveness of the purchase.

Impulse—that was a concept Stone's disciplinarian father systematically sought to eliminate in his only child. The man did his work with typical thoroughness. Stone's parents had died the summer before his junior year at Yale, and, other than the on-the-spot purchase of Penuche, Stone hewed to the program his father laid down: Yale, football, the Army, law school. Never had he permitted himself a private reflection on this path; he walked through it as though it were ordained—which, in a way, it was. Stone's father had performed the ordination.

Stone found himself a second-year law student at Harvard the day the lightning metaphorically hit home. His superb grades guaranteed him a clerkship with a U.S. Supreme Court Justice upon graduation. That was his father's agenda.

Penuche was sitting on Stone's outstretched forearm the day that agenda was scrapped. They were sitting in Jack's Bar on Massachusetts Avenue in Cambridge, just a few blocks from the shadows of the law school. Stone had his Beck's beer before him; Penuche, his saucer of water. The cockatoo's patch of skin on his cheeks suddenly turned from its normal pink shade to a deep red, the coloration that indicates the bird is angry or excited. Stone, if he had a visible mood-indicating patch, would have revealed the same sharp change, for it was Stone whom Penuche was reacting to.

Poof! Stone drained his beer, stroked Penuche's crest, and walked out of Jack's. He never returned. He had determined to derail his father's elaborate plans and become his own man.

But those were events of yesteryear. Stone did not reflect on his transformation from a drab pin-striped lawyer-to-be into an international gunslinger. That did not worry him. The change in Penuche's cheek-patch color did.

"You're revealing yourself, Penuche," Stone kidded. "Don't you wish you didn't show all your feelings?"

"Leah!" the bird croaked, and the patch turned still darker red.

"That's right," Stone replied. At times he felt silly talking to Penuche—the bird could mimic a hundred or so words but understood not a syllable. Still, Stone found the bird's talkative presence comforting as he sorted through plans and options. "I got it," Stone said, smiling as he fed Penuche a few sunflower seeds. "You think a mission is coming up because of Leah." Stone knew Penuche hated being parked in the "bird hotel" where he left him when a mission drew Stone out of town. Stone had to admit it: He found the bird's affectionate, if fierce, attachment to him touching. "Well, 'Nuche, old buddy, let's hope you're wrong. A policeman I'm not, and this Turin caper is police work, pure and simple. Let's hope, Penuche."

Penuche's cheek patch provided the bird's rejoinder. It remained bright red.

"Salvatore DiGrazia, please," the voice said.

"May I say who's telephoning him," Sophia screened the caller. DiGrazia ordinarily accepted every call that came in—when he proclaimed his door stood open, he meant it. But this Monday morning Sophia decided to wedge that door shut. Her boss had far more urgent problems on his mind than minor complaints from Especiale owners.

"He'll talk to me. If, that is, he wants to see his daughter alive."

Sophia patched the call through.

"Salvatore DiGrazia speaking."

"This is the Seventh Mao Force, DiGrazia. We have your daughter. Fifty million bucks, in American cash, buys her back. Period. We will not negotiate. Your money or her life, it's that simple. Are you buying?"

"Of course, of course." DiGrazia inwardly reeled at the immensity of the sum. His Maria was worth that and more, but could DiGrazia raise that much in a short time span? "How long do I have to raise the cash?"

"Five days, DiGrazia. Five days from today Maria walks away free. Or we dump the body."

"No!" DiGrazia refused even to imagine Maria's corpse. "You will get your money. But—" DiGrazia's more cautious instincts asserted themselves. He had heard of it before. When tragedy strikes a family, poseurs and psychotics by the droves climb out of the sewers to pester the sufferers. Could this be an indescribably obscene prank, he wondered. "How do I know you have Maria and that she's alive?"

"DiGrazia, your job is to do what we tell you. *Not* to ask questions. You don't know that Maria is alive, and the SMF gives a fuck about it. But we definitely kidnapped her, asshole." The question peeved Teresio. He had scripted the conversation before calling to guard against slips of the tongue. That DiGrazia might doubt his authenticity did not occur to him. "Her car. I know where it is." After Teresio pinpointed the location of the custom-built Especiale, he could not deny himself a kick at this industrialist whom he knew was down. "Her panties, DiGrazia. They're white," Teresio leered into the mouthpiece. "At least they were before last night," he cackled.

DiGrazia winced. Give me this guy for five minutes, he wished. Five minutes alone. But he wisely stifled his anger. "How do I get the money to you?"

"You'll get another call. You will be told. And, DiGrazia, keep the cops out of this. If we so much as see a cop in our neighborhood, the girl's throat is slit. Got it?"

Teresio slammed down the receiver when DiGrazia assented. The police, DiGrazia thought to himself. He would gladly keep them out. They would do no good anyway. But $50 million? The preposterous unreality of the demand staggered him. Maybe my accountants have a solution, DiGrazia hoped. Maybe.

Maria, too, found herself searching for solutions in her closet cell. Her stomach rumbled; she had not eaten since yesterday's toast. But she knew better than to try calling her kidnappers by banging on the door. The man, the nut, could do anything, she feared, and in the closet she was at least safe from him. For how long she wondered.

Long. The concept of time ceased to make sense to Maria in her prison. She measured time not by the hour —in her pitch-black cell the clock did not matter—but by the intensity of her hunger pangs and the sharpness of the pains in her bladder. She had not relieved herself since before the kidnapping. She squeezed her legs tight. Counting the cockroaches that infested the closet distracted her from her discomforts, but that task proved dizzying in the darkness. Even so, the roaches afforded a perversely welcome amusement—they took her mind off her miseries. So far, she thanked the lord, although she shared their floor and her hand and feet bindings prevented her from shooing them away, the roaches nonetheless seemed inclined to avoid her. But she had to go to the bathroom . . . so badly.

"Good morning." Gina opened Maria's door, and a brief but friendly smile crossed her face. With Teresio out contacting DiGrazia, Gina had decided to investigate the comfort of their victim. Maria's circumstances could not be pleasant, Gina realized, but she intended to make them as tolerable as she could.

Maria welcomed the intrusion. She liked the girl. A terrorist she might be, but she has already saved me from the man, Maria reflected. When Gina removed the gag from her mouth, Maria's thanks were profuse. Feel her out about freeing me, Maria's inner-voice rumbled. Now. Ask her. But when Maria spoke, her requests were more concrete.

"I hate to trouble you. But" —Maria's bladder bordered on bursting—"I need to go to the bathroom. Soon."

Gina understood and, after explaining the building's lack of plumbing, fetched Maria an empty wine jug and undid her hands. She knew Vincent never would have approved, but she also closed the door to grant Maria a measure of privacy. Vincent, Gina thought to herself, probably would have watched the girl piss. The pervert! Some moments she hated him, saw him as a male pig of the worst kind. Then she would catch herself liking him again. Their friendship went deep, too deep to be disrupted by a bad day or two.

"Here's a bite of bread and some water," Gina said as she handed the provisions to Maria and retrieved the wine jug. It was nearly full, almost a liter high, Gina noticed, and felt another twinge of sorrow for the girl who had done nothing to warrant this treatment, except be born into a wealthy family. "I'm sorry. Bread and water are all we have."

"That's appropriate for a prisoner," Maria, her spirits on the rise, joked.

Gina had to laugh. She did not think she could be cracking jokes were she the prisoner. "Glad to see you're feeling okay."

"I'm not," Maria confessed. "It's awful in here. No light, no toilet, and a million roaches for roomies. But . . . at least I'm alive."

Gina heard the unstated question. Everyone in Italy could recite the horror stories of husbands who ransom kidnapped wives, parents who ransom children, sons who ransom mothers—and won only the return of a corpse. The dead make bad witnesses and once a kidnapper has the loot in hand, extinction of the best eyewitness of all—the victim—routinely follows. Still, the families pay. They knew all this and knew, too, that refusal to pay absolutely ensures the death of the abducted loved one. Pay your money and take your chances, that's the rule—the only sure one.

"We— I intend to keep you alive, Maria. If your father comes through, you go free. That's a promise."

"I like you, Gina," Maria said simply. "When this is over, perhaps we can be friends."

"Sure, Maria." Gina did not believe it, but she was glad Maria said it. "Sure."

A rumbling up the stairs put a halt to this conversation. Gina could not decide if she should pick up her AK-47—it might be the cops, she thought—or stow Maria back in the closet for safer keeping when Vincent's around. Fuck it, she decided. If it's the cops, the gun will make no difference. I don't want to pull the trigger. Ever.

"Back in the closet," Gina whispered. Maria eagerly followed her advice. It was away from the man.

"How's our prisoner of war," Teresio asked when he entered to see Gina bolting the closet door.

"I just checked. She's fine. How did the call go?"

"That shithead! He wanted to hear my bonafides, like I'm not the one with the power. I mean, who has his fucking bitch of a daughter?" Teresio still sizzled over DiGrazia's question about his authenticity. "But," Teresio gloated, "I have him by the balls and he knows it. Fifty million bucks' worth, I have him."

"He's going to pay?" Gina inquired skeptically.

"Bet your ass, Gina. Grab a man by his balls and his wallet is sure to follow. Maybe Mao said that. He should have. Anyway, I gave him five days. Even a rich prick like DiGrazia can't wave a wand and make that kind of cash magically appear. Give him five days, and he can definitely get it together. Besides, he has no choice."

"Once we get the money, then what? What comes next," Gina probed.

"We continue the revolution. Play it by ear," Teresio evaded her questions. He knew exactly what came next, but Gina no longer figured into his plans. Well, he admitted to himself, maybe she did. After yesterday's fight, he was no longer sure. But he was sure that, once DiGrazia's money lined his torn pockets, he would be fast on his way out of Italy. Ditch Maria, that's the first step Teresio had decided. Can't leave her to point a finger at me. Hop a plane and head out, maybe to Los Angeles in the United States. He had seen that city in movies and figured, what with its fast-cash glitzy culture, an Italian newcomer with lira to spend could fit right in. Shit, perhaps he would become a movie producer and put his money to work making more money. Toss in a left-wing twist to the plots of the movies and, bamm!, the conscience stays happy while the bank account swells.

"Did you ever think of making movies, Gina? Ones with revolutionary themes, I mean, like Jean-Luc Godard's? We'll have the cash to do it."

What a wild idea, Gina mulled. Smart-crazy, not crazy-crazy. Millions of people see movies. That's millions who can be alerted to and aroused by the economic injustices of capitalism, the rotting of our art, the destruction of our air and water. "Wow! Where'd you come up with that, Vin? I like it. I really do."

They smiled and, for the first time in a long day, felt close to one another. They liked the feeling.

"Good news, Mr. DiGrazia. We've found your daughter's car," Chief DelRay announced.

Salvatore DiGrazia groaned silently. Would the police be excited enough by this break to actively pursue the case? More critically, did the location coincide with the address pinpointed by the SMF caller?

When DelRay identified the spot where the car had been found, it satisfied DiGrazia's second concern. The legitimacy of the fifty-million-dollar ransom demand could no longer be doubted. The first worry lingered.

DelRay exacerbated it. "But here's the best news. My lab men tell me there are fingerprints all over the car. Once they put them through our terrorist identification units, we'll have firm IDs on your daughter's kidnappers. I promise you, Mr. DiGrazia, we will have this case closed by nightfall."

Salvatore DiGrazia had heard that timetable before. Yesterday, DelRay's prediction turned sourer than month-old ricotta cheese. But, maybe, DiGrazia hoped, maybe this chief is better than his bureaucratic predecessor who cared only for the smooth passage of time on the way toward collecting a fat pension. Perhaps . . .

DelRay broke into DiGrazia's reflections. "Meantime, Mr. DiGrazia, we're rounding up every suspected terrorist in Turin. When that ID comes through, the culprits will already be in custody." DelRay gloated at this clever *pièce de résistance* he had concocted. It would take the heat off him—heat that had topped the melting point when the DiGrazia kidnapping capped a week that began with the Turin Post Office bombing and hit stride with the murders of Chief Albanese and his wife. The press, the mayor, the voting citizens of Turin would adore this plan to stifle further terrorist acts by undertaking a preemptive strike against likely bombers, kidnappers, and killers.

DiGrazia's pain throbbed through the phone lines. "Chief, if you arrest a single member of the Seventh Mao Force, my daughter dies. The others will kill her. I know that."

This protest startled DelRay. The man's daughter is kidnapped, and he wants to go soft on terrorists in our town? It makes no sense. DelRay sought time to sort out this bemusing development. "Hold on, Mr. DiGrazia. Don't be pessimistic. Like I said, when the prints come back from the lab and flow into our computers, we'll have your daughter back and she will be safe and sound. I'm sure of it."

When the conversation closed on that note, DiGrazia ceased to waver. He promptly put in a call to his accountant. The call produced only more bad news: "Fifty million? It cannot be done, Mr. DiGrazia," the accountant reported sadly. Even if Especiale were sold lock, stock, and carburetor, outstanding indebtedness would eat up the bulk of the proceeds. The net would hit $40 million at most, the accountant's calculator printed out. "Assuming Especiale is not sold," the depressing litany continued, "five million dollars is within reach—not a cent more."

The financial balance sheet did not surprise DiGrazia. He had anticipated this news . . . but the tragedy it boded for Maria nonetheless momentarily knocked the spirit out of him. Perhaps, DiGrazia considered, he should have run his business and his personal financial affairs differently. Had not his accountants always insisted that he lived too close to the bone?

But DiGrazia's indulgences were not the caviar, cocaine, and champagne of the monied continental jet set. He rewarded his employees with the finest pay package in Italy. He demanded that every Especiale part be of the highest-grade materials; there was no scrimping of the sort that saw other automobile makers' cars disintegrate into hissing piles of worthless rubble once the last monthly installment payment arrived at the bank. And when Turin's charities called on Especiale and DiGrazia, he did not hand them a few lira while rushing them out the door. DiGrazia welcomed them and gave generously. He dug especially deep for his pet charity: a maternity ward for Turin's poor. If DiGrazia had his way, no more husbands would lose their wives in childbirth. His dollars by the thousands flowed regularly to this maternity ward to make that wish a reality. Add up the totals, as DiGrazia's accountants had, and there was no denying that DiGrazia lived well, but there was also no denying that many, many others in Turin lived better because of his efforts.

"It's him again. Chief DelRay," Sophia announced over DiGrazia's intercom. He instantly grabbed the phone.

"Mr. DiGrazia?" the chief's voice purred irritatingly into the phone. "Bad news, I'm afraid." DiGrazia's heart tightened.

DelRay rushed on: "The fingerprints provided no good clues." The damn lab, DelRay muttered to himself. The only prints they lifted off the car belonged to the kidnapped girl and the Turin cop, who found the car and evidently treated himself to a spin in it before notifying headquarters of his discovery. "We're back at square one. I'm sorry."

"What about the arrests of suspected terrorists? How's that proceeding, Chief?"

"Fine. Very fine," DelRay lied. He cursed his men: So far, not a single terrorist had been booked. In a city crawling with criminals, his patrols could not find even a pickpocket to arrest and parade before the press as the prime suspect in the post office explosion.

"Oh." DiGrazia's optimism dissolved. "Any SMF members under arrest?"

"I'm afraid not," DelRay reported honestly. "They are very professional. But we'll nab them soon. We're extremely close to a major arrest. I'll keep you fully informed." DelRay rushed to close the conversation before it revealed the total lack of progress his men had made. "I'll be back soon with good news. You can bet on it."

DiGrazia gladly let the chief ring off. He knew the only news DelRay would bring would be the report of the discovery of Maria's festering corpse. But at least the police are backing off DiGrazia surmised. Their continued fumbling intervention could bring only tragedy, and it was a tragedy DiGrazia meant to avoid.

"Salvatore, here's lunch. You must eat," Sophia said as she carted in a tray laden with bread, provolone, mortadella, and a pot of espresso. DiGrazia plunged into his food; he had not eaten since Maria's kidnapping, he remembered. Nourishment might rekindle his withering imagination, provide a clue as to where to look for the outside help that surely would be required to save Maria's life. The thought of his daughter's premature death threatened to foreclose his appetite.

"Eat, Salvatore. You must keep up your strength," Sophia mothered him. She loved her boss—like a good friend. DiGrazia, she knew, reciprocated in kind. That is why, try as she did, Sophia could not entirely mask her feelings: "Salvatore, what can we do? How can I help? I must."

"I wish I knew what to say, Sophia. Where can I turn? The Turin police? Ha! They will only get Maria killed with their bungling officiousness. Private detectives? The best security agency in Turin guarded her when she was kidnapped. I must bargain with this Seventh Mao Force; it is my only hope. They must understand, I cannot raise their fifty million. I will pay what I can. Everything. Anything. We must trust in their reasonableness. Meantime, we can pray."

CHAPTER 6

DiGrazia did not welcome the arrival of the second day: His five days, the time granted him by the Seventh Mao Force, grew painfully shorter with each passing second. Time, DiGrazia felt, ticked toward an alarm; when it rang, Maria died.

But the ringing he heard was not that alarm. It was his home telephone. He rose from a tormented sleep.

"DiGrazia?" The voice growled.

"Here." Salvatore DiGrazia could muster no better, not when each call brought worsening news.

"When you get the money, we want it in small bills. Nonconsecutive serial numbers. No fuckups, DiGrazia."

"Maria? How is she?"

"Your rich-bitch daughter? How do you think I got your phone number? She's breathing. That's all you need to know."

Should I tell him, DiGrazia fretted. Will he just kill Maria now if I do? DiGrazia, knowing that failure to deliver the agreed-upon ransom would seal Maria's death, opted to take the chance and try to negotiate the payoff downwards. "I cannot raise fifty million dollars. It is impossible."

Teresio's anger erupted. "Fuckhead! Do *not—never!—* give me that line of shit. I am *not* one of your stupid workers to whom you plead poverty when it comes time to give pay raises. I know you and I know Especiale,

DiGrazia. You don't think we investigate before planning an action? Give me more shit and—"

DiGrazia hurried to interrupt the angrily sputtering voice. Had he known that the SMF's "investigation" consisted of a single newspaper story Teresio had read months ago, he might have acted differently. But DiGrazia could not know that. He knew only that each venomous syllable uttered by the kidnapper made Maria's tenuous hold on life still more slippery. "I beg you. I'll get the money. I will," DiGrazia implored the cursing voice to curtail its stream of homicidal torture.

"Damn right you will. Give me one more ounce of crap, DiGrazia, and you'll be getting a present in the mail. Maria's tits. The rest of her, what's left when we're done, will go down the Turin sewers. Got it?"

DiGrazia reined in his cresting tide of anger. His assent nonetheless was sincere; the alternatives were too horrible to contemplate.

"That's a good boy, capitalist swine. You're a dumb shit, but you're learning." Teresio relished his opportunity to pour verbal sulfuric acid into DiGrazia's open wounds. But much as he delighted in tormenting "this representative of the gluttonous greed of the capitalist state"—as Teresio characterized DiGrazia to Gina—he knew he could not prolong these sadistic bouts. Tracers on the calls could put the police on him within minutes. To foil those traces, he had coerced the DiGrazia home number out of Maria, but Teresio knew he could not depend on a pattern of random calls to evade that electronic net. "The next call will tell you where to deliver the money, DiGrazia." Teresio signed off. He had also, quite inadvertently, made up DiGrazia's mind.

"No calls this morning, Sophia," DiGrazia ordered upon entering his office. "Particularly no calls from DelRay." Keep the chief at bay; that was DiGrazia's first firm decision. The second was to put Maria's fate solidly in his own hands. He could not meet the ransom demand. That was clear. But DiGrazia knew other avenues could be pursued; direct action could be instigated. This morning he intended to unearth those avenues. There would be someone, somewhere, who could help, DiGrazia knew. He sat himself down at his desk for a busy day of poring through old papers and files in search of the hidden but essential clue.

"The bastard," Teresio fumed when he climbed back to his hide-out. "You know what he said, Gina? He told me *he*, Salvatore DiGrazia and the owner of the filthy-rich Especiale company, could not raise the fifty million. The pig! He would sell his best friend for forty pieces of silver—but won't buy back his daughter."

"The deal's off, Vin?" Gina's optimism bounced skyward. Did this signal an end to the whole messy business? An escape hatch?

"Naw. The asshole! After I told him what we'd do to his daughter, he came through. The little shit was just trying to talk down the price. The money will be ours, I'm sure of it. Hell, it would be bad public relations for a fat-cat tycoon to write off his only child like a bad investment. Which reminds me, how's she doing?"

Before Gina could contrive an excuse for keeping Teresio away from Maria, he marched to the closet, undid the lock, and opened the door. Maria stood before him with neither hands nor feet bound.

Jump him, a part of Maria whispered. Kick him in the groin, just like they teach in self-defense class. Then run for the outside door—and freedom.

"What gives, Gina?" Teresio put an end to Maria's idyll of escape by firmly grabbing her flowing hair and yanking her head out of the closet.

"I untied her, Vin. She can't even piss with her hands and feet tied, and with the lock on the door she can't escape anyway."

"Fuck her, Gina. Let her piss on the floor, drown a few roaches." Teresio, fact is, cared nothing for the roaches; cockroaches had been a staple in his life since childhood. What he did care about was finding time alone, just him and the rich kid. He would show her what poor boys could do. Yes, indeed, Teresio smiled.

"It would stink, Vincent, and the whole damn place would start to smell. It's no big deal, letting her stay untied," Gina said, matter-of-factly dismissing his contentions. "She is our prisoner. We owe her a few courtesies at least." Untied hands were one. Both Gina and Teresio knew the other, unspoken one was freedom from probing hands.

Time alone with her; that's all Teresio cared about right now. His mind groped for a way. "Gina, you're better at shoplifting than I am," Teresio complimented his partner. "We've got to eat. How about heading down to Balducci's and liberating some cheese and bologna?"

It was true. They had not a morsel of food left in the hide-out. But could Gina trust Teresio with Maria?

Sensing her hesitation and its underlying reasons, Teresio hurriedly shoved Maria back into the closet and securely locked the door. "You're right, Gina. We owe her a little courtesy. Her hands and feet can be untied."

Gina accepted his tacit message. What choice did she have? Food had to be gotten. "Okay, Vincent. I'll see what I can scrounge up at the store."

At first glance the name elicited no response from DiGrazia. His attention had blurred, and hundreds of papers lay scattered about him. But this one intrigued him. Leah Aviv? An international public relations consultant? He knew he had never hired her—Especiale employed no PR staffers to flack its wares. The car spoke for itself; and the company's deeds in the community, DiGrazia resolved long ago, were not done to win press coverage. He and Especiale did what they did because they had to, not to garner public recognition. But how did this card get in his files, DiGrazia wondered. Then it hit him, as memories of enigmatic late-night car loans to a beautiful Israeli spy flickered past his eyes. A woman spy? What could she do in these circumstances? With all his hopes nearly gone anyway, DiGrazia decided to take this wild stab. The London phone number rang.

"Leah Aviv."

"Hello," DiGrazia began awkwardly. He knew no precedents for such a conversation. "This is Salvatore DiGrazia. Perhaps you remember me."

Leah, too, was at a loss for words. Her long-distance

investigation into the SMF had yielded no fruit, nothing at all to lift the spirits of her caller. "I remember, Mr. DiGrazia," Leah offered softly.

"My daughter," DiGrazia started out. "She—"

Leah recognized the signs of a strong man's voice cracking under enormous strain. Her own voice waded in to soothe his sufferings. "I know about Maria and the Seventh Mao Force, Mr. DiGrazia. I've kept up with the details in the newspapers and . . ." Leah paused to give herself time to decide how much she should confide in Salvatore DiGrazia. He had not betrayed past confidences, but S-COM's business is of a different, a more delicate and less sanctioned sort than that of official government agencies. "Tell me, Mr. DiGrazia, how close are the police to solving the case?" She knew the answer before asking, but by asking she bought herself more time.

DiGrazia supplied the answer in one brusque word: "Never! The Turin Police are incapable of handling it. The life of my daughter is at stake, Miss Aviv. Those bunglers can only cost her her life. That"—DiGrazia recovered his composure—"is why I am calling you. To see if, how do I say, your unorthodox channels might provide a better hope. You are out of that business and into public relations, according to your business card, but can you recommend a firm that is versed in handling these sensitive affairs?"

DiGrazia's direct approach ended Leah's quandary. "I think so, Mr. DiGrazia. There is an excellent team . . . the world's best, many say. Kidnappings, however, are a bit out of their line. But I would welcome acting as your go-between to determine their interest. This, Mr. DiGrazia, I know for a fact: Nobody can do a better job. But I cannot promise they will accept it. I wish I could be more encouraging."

"The truth is refreshing, Miss Aviv. Much better than the hollow assurances I have been getting."

"You will get nothing but the truth from this group, Mr. DiGrazia. And if I have any influence on them, they will be helping you within hours. If, that is, I have influence," Leah cautiously underlined. Only Stone could commit S-COM, Leah knew. "Give me one hour. I'll know by then."

Maria greeted the rustling of the lock on her closet door with enthusiasm. She eagerly looked forward to another talk with Gina. This time she meant to ask for her freedom.

But it was not Gina at the door. It was Teresio; as soon as he was certain Gina had departed to get food, he dashed to the closet.

It was with horror that Maria saw Teresio entering her closet. The horror deepened when, yanked out, she instantly detected Gina's absence. "Gina. Where is she?"

"None of your fucking business." Teresio dragged her over to the mattress. "Now we'll finish that interrogation I started Sunday, bitch." Teresio's hands grabbed her wrists; he pressed his lips hard against Maria's. She could feel his erection swelling against her as his mouth covered hers and his tongue unyieldingly pressed downward into her throat.

Teresio could sense it; Maria's struggle lessened as he persisted in his advances. He knew it. He had been certain she would be a willing lover. Teresio relaxed his tight grip on her wrists and, then, feeling completely confident of his romantic charms, freed her entirely. His hands rushed to caress the breasts he had coveted for lengthy hours.

Their kissing went on for minutes. Foreplay, Teresio philosophized, is the key to successful lovemaking. He relished it, doted on every moment spent in preparatory exploration of his partner's body. Maria, he could tell, shared his enthusiasms. Her hands deftly glided over his body and gently massaged tense muscles as they passed by.

Maria's hands dove to Teresio's waist. She undid his zipper and Teresio tensed in anticipation of her initial touch of his massive erection. It would please her; he knew it was a solid one.

His kisses dove deeper as he felt Maria tugging his pants down. He basked in his sensuality and thrilled in her sensuousness. Her body delighted him with its bountiful curves, its taut fullness. When he began to unzip her skirt, he felt Maria's hands seeking his penis. Then her fingers cupped his testicles. A dream, that's what this is, Teresio thought.

It turned into a nightmare. Maria had digested the chief lesson in her self-defense class: A man's most vulnerable spot is his testicles. When her grip was good, Maria squeezed. She exerted every ounce of strength she could muster and just kept squeezing, tighter and harder, on Teresio's testicles. She could feel the soft balls within his scrotum flattening. Teresio's agonized shrieking did not deter her. Then she flashed into unconsciousness.

Teresio, feeling his own consciousness ebbing away and the pain in his groin soaring in immensity, had instinctively flailed at his attacker. A wild shot became a haymaker. Maria's grip relaxed, and as it did, Teresio felt—amidst the continuing pain—his consciousness returning. He saw her prone body lying still.

"Holy shit! Gina!" Teresio heard the footsteps starting up the stairs. He knew he was in neither the mood nor the shape to explain away this incident, not that he understood why Gina cared at all if he raped the girl. But she cared, he knew; probably jealousy, he suspected. He speedily pulled up his pants and dragged the unconscious Maria back to her cell. Just as he locked the door shut, he heard the voice.

"Vincent! What the fuck are you doing!"

"Nothing, Gina. Nothing's the matter. I heard a noise in the cell, that's all. Thought I'd better investigate. You know what? The bitch was trying to lift up a floorboard. Smacked her a good one and kicked the board down solid. No way she's going to get out."

Gina swallowed his explanation, and Teresio patted himself on the back for that tale. Damn, my nuts hurt. It will be a pleasure killing that rich cunt, he thought. A definite pleasure.

"What's to eat? I'm starved," Teresio said.

"So DiGrazia called you, Leah? I wish S-COM could help. But this is a kidnapping. It's a matter for the police, not a commando group."

"Stone, you know the track record of the Italian police. All they find is corpses—and only the ones terrorists like the SMF conspicuously leave for them to discover. It's this simple, Stone: If S-COM passes on this, the girl dies. I don't want that on my conscience. And every bit as much as you, I want to show terrorists—all of them—that they can be beaten. Direct, covert action, that's what will save the girl's life. The bureaucratic time-wasting of police departments won't. It's up to us, Stone."

Leah's argument appealed to Stone. This case provided a rich opportunity for testing out the theories he had developed for his Anti-Terrorist game. Besides, Stone sensed that if S-COM nixed involvement, Leah might free-lance this one. Leah's private life was her own concern; Stone knew he could not command her to drop the DiGrazia business. But he knew too that he definitely did not want Leah to face the dangers of Turin alone.

"We'll do it," Stone snapped. "*If* suitable financial arrangements can be made with DiGrazia. We are definitely *not* going into the mercy mission business," Stone stressed. "There will be our fee plus all expenses. Will he agree to our terms?"

"Yes, yes, Stone." Leah's happiness sped across the ocean via the underwater telephone cables. It was so strong, Stone could almost touch it. "I'll call him to say you'll be in touch with the details of S-COM's involvement. See you in Turin, Stone." Leah hung up.

"Squawk! Stone!"

"You guessed it, Penuche. Sorry, old boy. Duty calls."

"Squawk!" The palm cockatoo sulked. Stone played with the bird's massively powerful beak to cheer him up and perhaps to cheer himself up while counting off the minutes it would take Leah to contact DiGrazia and clear the way for Stone's call.

"We'll be back in a few days, Penuche," Stone promised as he lifted his phone and dialed DiGrazia. But Penuche, for one, remained unconvinced: His cheek patch flamed its deepest red. That unsettled Stone—it fed his own doubts about the wisdom of entangling S-COM in conventional police work—but he nonetheless waded into his spiel to DiGrazia.

"Mr. DiGrazia? This is Stone Williams. I represent Strategic Commandos. S-COM for short. You're in the market for our help?"

DiGrazia plunged into a recounting of his daughter's plight. Stone knew the facts, but he gave DiGrazia ample time to spin his tale. He wanted a sense of the man who stood to become S-COM's next employer. And he liked what he heard. DiGrazia's honesty helped to ease some of the trepidation that filled Stone.

"One question, Mr. DiGrazia," Stone interrupted as DiGrazia's flow reached its end. "Have you had contact with the Seventh Mao Force since the kidnapping?"

DiGrazia's hesitation in answering worried Stone, he would *never* work with an employer who held back facts—and that rule applied to everyone, the tight-lipped CIA included. But after lingering seconds ticked by, DiGrazia passed this test: "Yes," he sighed. "I've not told the police. Maria will die if even one SMF member is arrested. They told me that. If I informed the police, they would surely barrel ahead and do who knows what? I couldn't risk it."

"That's good policy, Mr. DiGrazia." Stone's satisfaction with the man continued to grow. He appreciated his initial reluctance to answer. But S-COM survived on the absolute trust of its members in one another—and in their employer. So far, DiGrazia had proved trustworthy. Stone proceeded to broach the second issue. "Our payment, Mr. DiGrazia, is cash in advance. S-COM does not work on a contingency fee basis; nor do we accept bonuses in the event of success. You understand that?"

DiGrazia did. Leah Aviv had briefed him fully on S-COM's unorthodox practices. But she had explained as well S-COM's guiding precept: If the group fails in a mission, S-COM dies also. Stone and the rest, if still breathing, would never unfurl the white flag of surrender. DiGrazia, who had seen Resistance fighters buckle in the face of totalitarian torture during World War II and had witnessed millions of contemporary Italians grow to passively tolerate terrorism as a deadly fixture on their nation's political landscape, admired this raw dedication to duty. And he welcomed Stone's terse toughness as a felicitous change of pace from the voluble cowardice of Police Chief DelRay.

"The fee," Stone continued, "will be five hundred thousand dollars. Upon our arrival in Turin, you will be provided with a list of five Swiss bank accounts to which you will forward one hundred thousand apiece." Stone, as always, divided the S-COM fee equally with the troops. As the commander, tradition entitled him to a heftier share of the take. But that practice, Stone believed, eroded morale among soldiers whose lives were every bit as much on the line as his. Besides, with his seven-figure inheritance and a steadily increasing income from electronic games, Stone did not need a penny of his S-COM wages. But he did not wish to be subject to the questions that inevitably would arise if he took no fee at all. So, an equal division it was—and always had been.

"Extraordinary expenses are additional," Stone appended to his money talk. Five- and six-figure bribes to government officials were a staple of Stone's business. Cash like that had more than once paved the way for S-COM to breeze into a nation with trunkloads of automatic weapons, mortar, and every other military armament up to—but not yet including—atomic devices. But in Italy Stone doubted such "additional expenses" would be required. Leah could use her copious Mediterranean contacts to arrange loans of whatever "black" weapons might be necessary. "Look forward to seeing you tomorrow, Mr. DiGrazia," Stone concluded.

DiGrazia almost broke into a jig when he cradled the telephone receiver. This man, Williams, meant business. Leah Aviv had given him the scantest background information on S-COM—security reasons, she explained, prevented painting a more detailed picture—but between the two of them, with Leah's obviously sincere concern for Maria's safety and Williams's no-nonsense approach, DiGrazia's spirits soared.

Sophia interrupted his premature ecstasy. "It's Chief DelRay on the line. He insists he must talk with you, that it's urgent news."

DiGrazia shivered. "Chief?"

"Good news, Mr. DiGrazia. You'll see it in the evening

newspapers and on television tonight, but I wanted to give you the word personally. We've made six major arrests of Turin terrorists. We're interrogating them now about your daughter."

"Are you positive that they're SMF members?" DiGrazia asked, his heart sinking.

"Definitely," DelRay beamed. "One man has a membership that dates all the way back to 1975. He's in their leadership; that's what our anti-terrorist squad tells me. But don't worry, Mr. DiGrazia, we have our techniques for cracking terrorists. They will all talk, you can count on it. The men remember what happened to Chief Albanese and his wife. The kid gloves are off in Turin. They will stay off as long as I'm chief."

DiGrazia could only hope against hope that DelRay had misidentified the SMF member. A single arrest meant Maria's corpse would be mailed to him parcel-post collect. That was a favorite terrorist stunt. When negotiations fell through, the victim was carved up and shipped back to the family in a small box. The arms, legs, torso—all are axed down to small bits. In Turin, no one greeted the delivery of an unexpected package with surprised delight. Not any more. It could be a friend or relative.

Strangely, however, not even DelRay's potentially fatal flubbing could thoroughly deflate DiGrazia. Not now. He had S-COM on his side, and while the group and its techniques remained a puzzle to him, the knowledge that they would soon be winging into Turin buoyed his spirits. Matters were slipping out of his hands . . . and into Stone Williams's. Complete control, that's what Stone insisted on. He would have it, DiGrazia determined, if somehow the blundering DelRay could be sidetracked from making that one, last error that certainly meant Maria's death.

"Progress, Salvatore?" Sophia asked when DiGrazia concluded his conversation with the chief. His improved mood had instantly communicated itself to her. Six years spent at DiGrazia's side enabled Sophia to read him at a glance.

"I think so, Sophia. But we won't know for sure until Friday." That marked the fifth and final day on the abbreviated calendar granted Maria by the kidnappers. As Tuesday night enshrouded Turin, Maria had just three more days to breathe. If, that is, DelRay's mindless meandering had not already provoked the terrorists into killing her. DiGrazia struggled to put that funereal imagery out of his mind. Sophia helped ease the way.

"Tonight I'm treating you to supper at my place, Salvatore. Stop right there," she said, taking control. "You're always treating me to dinner. It's my turn."

"I'd love to, Sophia, but—"

"No but's, Salvatore. Nobody can deal with these stresses on a perpetually empty stomach. Not even you," she said.

Maybe it *would* do me good, DiGrazia agreed. There's nothing more I can do for Maria tonight. Her fate is in the hands of God—at the mercy of the SMF. *Tomorrow*, however, that changes—tomorrow, when S-COM arrives in Turin.

"I'd be delighted, Sophia." DiGrazia again praised the twists of fate that had plunked Sophia at his door in search of a job. She came to Especiale, she told him, because of its reputation. Secretaries at Especiale were not treated the way they were at other Turin companies; the low pay and contemptuous treatment that afflict most women in the "pink-collar" positions were absent at Especiale. DiGrazia had immediately admired her spunk, and after a probationary period in the sales department, Sophia got promoted to the post of DiGrazia's personal secretary. She was more than that, he knew: a valued assistant, a beloved friend. He knew he could count on Sophia to stand by him. She never failed.

Nor did her veal Marsala fail that night. DiGrazia's dormant appetite awoke with a roar as he savored the tender meat medallions and mopped up the delicate wine sauce. It was perfection. "Delicious, Sophia. You will make the man who marries you blissfully happy—and I'll be the first to serve as a reference."

Sophia soaked up his compliments. Her good looks, in fact, had earned her fistfuls of marriage proposals. Her cooking was a surprise that sweetened the pot. But at twenty-seven, and like many young women of her talents and age in every nation, Sophia had not yet inscribed a wedding in her agenda. Someday perhaps. But for now, she aimed to develop her talents and—just as importantly—enjoy the freedom her youth and generous Especiale salary afforded. "That will come, Salvatore. In due time."

"Careers come first with women these days. That's a big switch," DiGrazia said. "But it's good. Good for Italy and for business. Just last week, Maria"—he skipped a beat when his daughter's name and its present implications hit him, but Sophia's steadily encouraging smile put DiGrazia back on track—"she began working on plans for a new Especiale production model. Her designs are excellent too."

"Like father like daughter," Sophia laughed.

"I hope so. I hope we—all of us—come through this okay. Not knowing, that's the hardest part . . . not even knowing how she was kidnapped. I—"

Sophia's memory snapped on that. "The camera! The one that covers your driveway and door. Has the film been developed, Salvatore?"

DiGrazia slapped himself hard on the forehead. "Forgive me, Maria. Forgive me."

The pair bolted from Sophia's to DiGrazia's villa and the neglected camera. Sophia once again had demonstrated her incalculable worth, and along the way, she proved it more by attempting to allay DiGrazia's mounting guilt. But he could not acquit himself. There might be clues on the film that would be instrumental in freeing Maria.

While DiGrazia retrieved the negative, Sophia's calls to photography labs unearthed one that—despite the lateness of the hour—agreed to work the night through developing the miles of footage. Just one or two clear frames, that's all DiGrazia wanted. It would take until the morning to find out if the film offered him those frames.

CHAPTER 7

Stone's numbers came up fast and sure. Myles, Lucky, Rod, and of course Leah—all were accounted for and, within hours, would be arriving in London for S-COM's rendezvous. That was another of Stone's inviolable rules: Every S-COM fighter had always to be reachable by telephone and ready, at a moment's notice, to fly anywhere Stone ordered. Stone had to smile at Myles's joke that he would soon have them wearing beepers on their belts like doctors. What Myles did not know is that Stone had considered precisely that. Only the awkwardness of explaining away the undisguisable and shrill beep had deterred Stone from making them a mandatory feature of the S-COM uniform. So far, Stone calculated, there had been no problems with rounding up the troops. But in this line of work a moment's notice is often more than is gotten—the employer wants and needs immediate action. Although S-COM had never suffered a failure—because of delays or any other reason—Stone demanded that the record remain unblemished. An alternative but instant communications system was another of his many back-burner projects. Stone would play with it until it was perfect. But not now. Now he rested on the plane to London, and his thoughts centered on Turin and what S-COM would find.

A police force that made, not solved, problems. That awaited them, but it was par for the course. DiGrazia would be delegated to deal with them. Handling the cops would also keep DiGrazia out of S-COM's way, and that was a bonus. But how many terrorists would S-COM have to "dispose of," as Stone euphemistically expressed such black matters. Who would choose the turf for the confrontation? The terrorists? Or S-COM? That's critical, Stone knew. Let the enemy pick the time and place of battle, and defeat is yours. While the streaming jet plowed closer to London, Stone's agile mind probed deeper into the nuances of the anticipated battles. His enjoyment of military strategy was immense. And this fight, Stone intuited, would represent a major change of pace from past S-COM actions.

"We're here, sir. Heathrow." The stewardess's nudge awoke Stone from his speculations. He expected S-COM to win again, but damn, he muttered, the solutions persisted in evading him. Logic, Stone insisted, is what wins battles. But this time he wondered if it would be intuition that carried the day.

"Stone! Great to see you!" Leah could not resist throwing her arms around Stone's lean frame. He hugged her back, and their embrace lingered until Myles interrupted the duet.

"Stone Williams! Since when do we mix business and pleasure?" Myles cracked between his smiling lips.

Stone did not smile. Was he mixing business and pleasure? Which was Leah? Another point he marked down for eventual resolution.

"Myles!" Stone boomed to break the tension his pal's too-close-to-the-bone witticism had caused. Then he put the slighter Myles in a bear hug and bussed his cheek.

"Damn! Queers are everywhere," Lucky tossed in, and the entire S-COM band burst into heart-felt laughter. To a man, and a woman, they were pleased to be back in the mercenary saddle. Ribald, even coarse humor lightened their working days, and Stone invariably encouraged a lightly loose atmosphere during noncombat hours.

"To Turin, gentlemen." Leah had arranged first-class passage for all, and amidst servings of caviar—"fookin' fish eggs," Rod complained, "taste like a Times Square whore smells"—and fast-flowing booze, banter flowed freely, too. Neither food nor drink nor jokes stopped

Stone from sketching the Turin deal, but the backgrounding lasted only five minutes. "Not much to work with, gentlemen. But it's all we have."

"That and one hundred grand apiece," Lucky blurted. "Just might plunk it down on an Especiale."

"More gems for me," Myles chipped in. His collection, funded by S-COM proceeds, long ago eclipsed the ten million–dollar mark in value. Plus, as Myles had pointed out to a quizzical Lucky, the investment potential of stones and precious metals is unbeatable. Last year alone, his horde increased twenty-five percent in worth.

"How about you, Rod? Gonna settle down and marry yourself a kangaroo," Lucky ribbed the Aussie.

"Fookin' Cuban," Rod muttered. Of all the S-COM fighters, his sense of humor was slimmest, and his skill with words most meager. But that fretted Rod not a bit. His skill lay where it counted most—in battle. "Commie faggots, that's what you Cubans are. Christ, even Castro shipped 'em out by the boatload because he couldn't stomach his own kind. Can't fookin' blame him. Not if you're typical."

"But, Rod, at least I 'fook' girls. You've never screwed anything that doesn't have a pouch," Lucky stung back.

Rod had no retort for that shot. Rod's sex life, they all knew, consisted of an expanding series of one-night stands, with prostitutes. That embarrassed the inarticulate Aussie, especially since Stone, Myles, and Lucky all scored high, and often, with women.

"No more booze," Stone intervened. Rod had never been able to take a sharp joke, Stone knew. "By the way, Rod, you still have your VC ears?"

The group dissolved again into friendly laughter. Stone saw keeping the internal peace as a major part of a commander's job; and when the soldiers are mercenaries who fought only for money and not for patriotism and the other standard reasons, the job escalates in difficulty. That's why Stone kept a stock of sure-fire one-liners, and the VC ear line always worked with Rod. But it was not a joke. Not hardly, Stone realized. On more than one instance during his Nam tour, Rod's fury had led him into slicing an ear or two off a Viet Cong corpse. His anger, often in reaction to the grossly inept leadership exerted by the Western nation generals, had much to feed on. Rod's ear collection grew fast. By the end of his tour, Rod sported enough ears to fashion a crude necklace—and, misunderstanding one of Stone's caustic comments, he did precisely that. Stomach wrenching as Stone found this display, he suffered it, and in time, VC ears became to S-COM what Dolly Parton's breasts are to Johnny Carson: a reliable laugh getter.

Leah, in the midst of the wild joking and wilder partying indulged in by her comrades, kept her distance. On most trips she joined right in and matched her male colleagues guffaw for guffaw. Her language could blister the paint off a case-hardened subway station toilet seat, Myles had once observed, and his analysis rang true. But en route from London to Turin, Leah kept her own company.

Her thoughts zeroed in on S-COM's chief problem upon touching down in Italy: Finding a terrorist in Turin is easy; finding the *right* terrorist is not.

Leah thought, too, of Stone and their airport hug. She had liked that. Stone's closeness reassured her. Did it do more than that, she wondered.

Stone's thoughts tracked much the same terrain as Leah's. Each mission brought the two closer. He had missed Leah; it had been too long since he last saw her. He wanted to see more of her, Stone did. But he also wanted to respect the memory of his late best friend. Issues of that complexity did not sort themselves out in Stone Williams's methodical mind in a flash. Nor could Leah make speedy resolutions in this area, Stone sensed. Even so, he pondered why he had been so adamantly against Leah's solo involvement in this Turin mess, a prospect he found so unsettling that he had opted to bring in the entire group. In the past, when S-COM members pursued free-lance work on their own time, he had acceptingly shrugged his shoulders. That was their business, he proclaimed, as long as it did not interfere with S-COM's. This time, Leah's time, was different. Exactly why, Stone could not yet say.

The landing in Turin provided Stone a welcome break

in his speculations. "Bedtime, gentlemen. And lady. Sack out until 0800 hours. We'll regroup then. Time now is of the essence. There are three days left on the DiGrazia girl's calendar. Then she is dead."

"News from the photo lab, Salvatore. It's not good, I'm afraid," Sophia reported. "The kidnappers wore masks. There were two of them, but there are no glimpses of their faces. They tell me you can't even tell if it's two men, two women, or what or who did the kidnapping. It was overcast that day, and the images are very dark and blurred. You tried."

"Get the film anyway, Sophia. I want to see that horror story for myself. I must."

"Are you sure, Salvatore? You cannot punish yourself for this."

"Maybe I can see more than the lab. Maybe S-COM can. I don't know. But I know this: The film is the best lead I can give S-COM."

DiGrazia sighed when Sophia left for the lab. It was, despite Sophia's bad news, a sigh of relief. S-COM had arrived, and his first meeting with its leader was already scheduled. His spirits were higher than they had been in the previous three long and nearly unendurable days. Wednesday, Thursday, Friday—DiGrazia clicked off the days that Maria had left.

Teresio's call interrupted DiGrazia's optimism. "Pig! It's me again."

"What now?" DiGrazia snapped. His patience with the kidnapper ran thin.

"Show respect, capitalist running dog. *I* don't have to take your shit. *You* take mine. Remember?"

DiGrazia remembered. Maria's life insured that.

"Got the money?"

"Friday I'll have it. It will take until then," DiGrazia lied as Stone Williams had instructed. String him along, Stone advised. Grant any concessions he demands. Try to play him into providing a lead on his location, but don't push it.

"I insist on talking to Maria before handing over the money. I need assurances that she is still alive." That was another Williams idea; S-COM needed to know that Maria lived in order to plan its attack, and better still, Stone figured it would soothe DiGrazia's naturally frazzled nerves.

"Asshole! I told you, no questions, and that includes demands. The SMF does *all* the asking," Teresio bellowed.

"Be reasonable. You are asking me to hand over fifty million dollars. Fine, I'll do it. But are the goods in perfect working order? Is Maria alive?" DiGrazia stuck to the scenario Stone dictated to him over the phone. Don't fight with him, but don't grovel either, Stone stressed. Be calm and try to calm him. If he's not totally insane, he will eventually see your point, Stone predicted.

"She's just 'goods' to you? That's all, you fucking rich shit?"

"No, no. But think about the analogy." DiGrazia found himself struggling hard to adhere to Stone's script. Every syllable, he feared, bordered on triggering Maria's death. But DiGrazia persisted nonetheless. "You would ask the same, I'm sure."

"No good, you fuckhead," Teresio sputtered. This call, he could tell, had gone awry. He had enjoyed his earlier calls to DiGrazia and the abuse he heaped on the fightless man. This time differed. Teresio knew that, but the reason why baffled him. He did not like the change.

"Just one brief conversation. Ten seconds. A 'hello, Papa.' That's all I'm asking for."

"Up yours!" Teresio screamed. But the vehemence ebbed. The man had a point; Teresio could deny it only so long. "No phone calls. That's out. What am I supposed to do, cart your damn daughter down the fucking street to a pay phone? With her photograph in every newspaper? Asshole, you think I call from my own home?"

At last the SMF caller behaved with an iota of reasonableness. DiGrazia felt the change in the conversation's drift. He himself hewed to a steady line. "Have her write me a note, then. That's not requesting much. A few words that prove she is alive."

Teresio spat out his response: "You'll get your fucking

note!" He slammed down the phone and cursed the damnable DiGrazia family. Pricks, all of them! he raged. But he would definitely get the last laugh, Teresio swore. That was still to come on Friday.

"It's you! I'm so glad to see you," Maria said when Gina unlocked her door.

"Not much longer now, Maria. Today's Wednesday. You'll be home Friday." But Gina had to know: "You always seem so happy. You can't be."

"I'm not. I'm scared and miserable. But you . . . you're such an improvement over *him.*" Maria transformed that last word into an oath. "The man."

"He's not so bad," Gina laughed. "He's not always like this. The tension— But I guess you know as much about that as anyone."

"He tried to rape me." Maria's tears flooded at the memory. "Yesterday. While you were out getting food."

"He what? Again? The pig. The goddamn sexist pig. He promised me. He would leave you alone, he said."

Maria told the details. Gina's disgust grew as the picture of Teresio's immature lust fleshed out. "The prick! That's all he is, a stupid prick. Listen to me, Maria, I will get him for this. I will." But how, Gina wondered. Should she let Maria go? Right now, while Teresio is out making a call to DiGrazia? No, Gina told herself. I'm every bit as involved in this as Teresio. We'd both go to jail for life: for the post office bombing, the Albaneses, and now the kidnapping. Money, that's what I need to get out of this catastrophe.

Gina saw herself in a trap. Money, lots of it, afforded the only escape. She would have to see the kidnapping through. She hated to do it to Maria, hated to have to keep her within Teresio's reach, but it was the only way. Only three more days; they both could take it. By Friday, Maria would be home. And Gina would be on her way out of Turin and out of terrorism. Out of Teresio's life, too? Him, she did not know about. His deceit, his piggery—they had to be paid back, Gina swore. But the time would come, she concluded. It would come soon.

"Are there any clues, any leads you've held back from us, Mr. DiGrazia?" Stone was concluding his meeting with DiGrazia. He liked the man, but disliked his information. There was little to go on and less time to do it in. "Damned kidnappings. Police matters, not military missions," Stone had said under his breath more than once in the course of this meeting.

"Just the phone calls and, of course, the film. It's nothing, Mr. Williams. Nothing."

"We've gone on less." Stone had to reassure the client. That was critical. A nervous employer interfered and made mistakes—errors which might cost lives. "There's time. Sooner or later, we will get lucky, or the terrorists will get unlucky. It always happens." Would it happen by Friday? That was the question in Stone's mind. He had no doubt the SMF would execute Maria on Friday if DiGrazia failed to deliver the ransom. If, that is, they had not killed her days ago.

"The film. I'll take it with me," Stone added.

"But it's worthless."

"Maybe not, Mr. DiGrazia. We have a technique or two we use in enhancing images. Clues are what's needed right now. The film is all we have. That and whatever Leah digs up on her rounds of the police and international intelligence agencies. Meantime, my men are out poking around Turin. Getting a feel for the terrorist turf. One last question: Is there anyone else who might be able to help, anyone who has talked to the terrorist on your behalf?"

DiGrazia pressed a button to summon Sophia. "My aide, Sophia Giacomo," DiGrazia said as Sophia entered the office.

Stone admired the turn of her body and welcomed the shyly bold smile that flashed across her face when she saw the handsome American soldier. "Pleased to meet you, Sophia. The name is Williams, Stone Williams."

At the University of Turin's snackbar, Lucky was making more direct headway with pretty Italian women. Students, particularly in the politically more turbulent nations, often are keen observers of the most radical organizations and an idle remark might give S-COM a lead straight into the SMF's lair. Lucky, the youngest of the troupe, had volunteered for the assignment, and Stone readily consented. Lucky's charms with women had paid off big dividends in past cases, and that was his technique in Turin: casually approach a pretty girl; buy her coffee; and get the woman talking. His halting Italian supported his pose as an exchange student from the University of Havana, and the mention of that alma mater also provided an instant entree into leftist circles that were keen on hearing an insider's view of the Cuban revolution.

Lucky played his part with gusto. Who knows, he considered, he just might succeed in bedding one of the more winsome coeds later that day. That hope, plus his quest for SMF leads, gave his fractured Italian a fluency of its own.

The burly soccer player who stalked up to Lucky had more on his mind than fractured Italian. It was bones he wanted to see broken, Lucky's bones. Lucky, it seemed, was making too fast time with the man's girl. Her flirtatious giggles, aimed at Lucky's smooth face, turned the soccer player's face red with boiling anger. His punch lashed out at Lucky's nose.

It did not land. Lucky, glimpsing the on-rushing haymaker, dove from his chair. He thudded on the floor; it hurt but less than his face would have been pained had the punch connected. The man, with only air to greet his fist, stumbled after his extending arm and into a chair.

Lucky sprang to his feet. He had no gun, but that lack concerned him not at all. Stone insisted that every S-COMer—save Rod, who needed no practice in street-fighting; Rod's hot temper won him far more bouts on the streets in a week than the rest of S-COM had in a year—regularly take lessons in a martial art. Lucky pursued karate, and he knew he could split the bigger man's head open as easily as he could cleave a two-by-four.

But the tension, the high stakes of the Turin mission, swamped Lucky's brain. He walked away from the sprawling and cursing soccer player. Neither he nor

S-COM, and certainly not Maria DiGrazia, could now afford a police investigation into a snackbar brawl. Contain your anger, Stone always preached. *Use* it; never wallow in it. Good as that dictum is, it was hard to remember. Even Stone recognized its practice proved elusive.

There would be no more to be learned on campus, Lucky determined. Not if he would have to spend the rest of his day fighting off the bruised soccer player and his brawny teammates. With a hurried goodbye to the man's lady friend, Lucky exited. He could only hope that the other S-COMers had had better luck.

Nil, no, and nothing. Those words greeted Leah at every intelligence agency she visited. Files on the SMF, where any existed at all, were dated, coffee-stained, heaps of idle speculation and idler gossip. But Leah had saved her best shot for last. If this route turned into a cul-de-sac, she would be back at "GO" without another throw of the dice.

"Leah. It's been years."

"Not since Tel Aviv, Dick. What brings you to Turin?"

"Exactly what I had in mind to ask you, Leah. But I'll go first. Terrorism, that's why I'm here. Italy is the international way station for terrorists of all nationalities. One big safe-house for them. I'm keeping tabs, following up the arms shipments, staying abreast of who is flying where, when, and how. Routine stuff."

Dick Konvitz perennially sold himself short, Leah knew. The number three man in Israel's burgeoning anti-terrorist squad, Konvitz followed the action. His world was never routine, although a less knowledgeable observer than Leah would have taken the drab man's word. Konvitz liked it that way. His low-profile insured that his work could proceed without too many questions being asked of him. Konvitz liked to do *all* the asking—and he knew everything. About everybody.

"How's Stone Williams," Konvitz asked, smiling. That had always been his style. The mark of a professional spook. He would not mention S-COM. It was, after all, illegal and—officially—had never and would never exist.

But Konitz's casual question served its purpose. It put Leah at ease. She knew and he knew that they both knew what was up in Leah's world, and because of that shared knowledge, there was no need to dwell on it.

"Fine. He keeps busy. Busier these days than most."

"Good to hear it." Konvitz meant it. Leah had told him that business, not a vacation, brought them to Turin, and her presence in Konvitz's office signaled that terrorism was the nature of that business. Unlike many professional spies, Konvitz welcomed help. Results, not jealous protection of means and information, were his only aim.

Leah welcomed his help, too. "The DiGrazia girl. Have you heard of her?"

Konvitz readily allowed that he had. His office followed every kidnapping, whether overtly political or not. They were all political at bottom, the Israeli's philosophy held: Money raised in an ostensibly nonpolitical body snatching often found its way into revolutionary coffers that in turn put the funds to use in buying weaponry that killed civilians, demolished buildings, and destabilized governments.

"The SMF is behind it, right, Dick?"

"Probably. But we're not certain, Leah. Odds are, yes. But the SMF slid into the deepest underground a few years back and only resurfaced with the post office bombing. Our assumption is that a handful of old-line SMF followers decided to hang out the old banner. But there are other possibilities. Two that we're considering. Could be there's a noncommunist group that's masquerading as the SMF or, maybe, just hard core criminals out for an easy score. Anyway, we've tossed around the notion that the kidnappers are from the Costello family. That Mafia bunch has been edged out of the American dope market by the Hispanics. They're desperate for cash, we hear, and this could be their way of raising money.

"Then, again, the Mussolini Federation could be the boys: a mean, dumb, right-wing crew of vulgar idiots who rail about the need for a return to Italy's 'old values,' whatever that might be. But DiGrazia has ruffled a lot of feathers in the big-money corporate community with his generous employment policies at Especiale. They've tried to persuade him to cut back on salaries and benefits, but the man's stubborn; he does as he chooses. Could be this is their way of breaking his back. Hit him up for a gigantic ransom, and whoosh, Especiale goes down the financial tubes.

"Add it up, however, and the SMF is still our top candidate. Right now, our people are going through the files on it. So far, nothing significant has come up. But if it does, I'll let you know."

"You have no hard leads on the SMF? Nothing concrete?" Leah prayed for at least a warm trail to sniff.

"Afraid not. Wait—There is a name . . . Teresio. Vincent Teresio. Two months ago an informant reported that this Teresio character—a nasty, unstable fellow, he told us—was circulating around college campuses trying to recruit new supporters for the SMF. Heard he had no luck, the SMF is ancient history to today's kids. The Red Brigades have a solid franchise on campus, even if the group is in its swan song because of all the recent arrests. Trouble is, all of that is from memory. When that report came in, it was deemed very low priority—just another burnt out and over-the-hill revolutionary nut looking for a band to lead. The file got misplaced, but we'll find it. Three secretaries are swimming through every scrap of paper in this ocean of paper work. It's there. It'll turn up."

"Call me the minute it does, Dick. Please." He would, Leah counted on it. Konvitz recognized the unspoken stakes of this game: Maria DiGrazia's life. His call would come. Leah could only hope it came in time.

They had drunk at lunch. Much too much, and Stone regretted the parting shots of anisette. Stone's talk with Sophia had produced nothing new, except Stone's passion. He found Sophia—her spunk and her sleek, swarthy good looks—immensely attractive. That's why he had proposed that they continue their talk back in his hotel room. Sophia had not objected.

All of which explained how Stone presently found himself tenderly nibbling Sophia's nipple while his hand explored the moistness between her legs. He moved his lips to her waiting mouth. Their kiss went deep, and with an assist from Sophia's darting left hand, his erection slid deep into her. With a singleness of purpose, they moved as one. Sophia met each of Stone's forward thrusts with one of her own as their pelvises rocked in sensuous unity. Faster, faster, Stone went, and Sophia's motions matched his in speed and intensity. He felt himself coming inside her, and seconds later, Sophia responded with a powerful orgasm of her own.

It had been good sex, Stone told himself. Very good. But Stone regretted it. A man of rules, he had violated the sternest rule of all laid down to S-COM members: Keep business and pleasure straight. Still, Stone rationalized, it definitely was pleasurable. That could not be denied. Nor could it be denied that his sex with Sophia eased Stone of some of the guilt he felt in regard to his feelings about Leah. And it helped, too, to put some distance between Stone and Leah, and Stone needed that now. Perhaps, he mulled, Leah did too.

Nonetheless, this was a pleasure he would not allow himself again—not until S-COM had recovered the DiGrazia girl and returned her to her father. Alive and well. Hell, Stone decided, perhaps this afternoon tryst was just as well. An assignment he at first disliked proved to have a rewarding fringe benefit, one that boosted his determination to solve the case. Soon. Stone wanted Sophia again and under more leisurely circumstances. It would have to wait. Until Friday.

"What do we have," Stone asked when his troops gathered later that day. Myles reported on the unproductive hours he and Rod had spent canvassing Italy's police agencies. "Chief DelRay. You should meet him, Stone. A real fookin' turd," Rod chimed in. Myles offered no dissent.

Lucky's report continued the discouragement. The high point of his day was the abortive fight with the soccer player at the University of Turin, and that brought S-COM no nearer to its goal.

Leah did not toss Stone the third strike he feared her turn at bat might produce. It was more a foul ball or, maybe, an infield dribbler. But Leah did marginally raise Stone's sagging spirits with her intelligence information and her report on the hardware friendly agencies had loaned: a half-dozen Heckler and Koch 9mm pistols and a like number of HK MP5 submachine guns; a pair of sawed-off Mercury 12-gauge magnum shotguns; and a box of Leah's personal favorites, the eight-pointed star-shaped shurikens favored by kung fu adepts.

"Christ, Leah. That's enough to put the whole damn city under siege," Myles joked.

"It already *is* under siege," Stone reminded. "The SMF has half of Turin afraid to step outside, and the other half is dead." Stone again remembered the ghastly image of the little girl in the post office. He could not shake that picture of the pretty head half blown away—not until the SMF had been splintered. "Two days. That's all we have left. Rod, tomorrow you check out the Costello family. Lucky goes after the Mussolini bunch. Myles takes the SMF. And let's hope Leah unearths fresh leads. Me, I'm going to babysit DiGrazia and check that film of his. There might be something on it. There better be."

"You chose wisely, Salvatore, when you hired S-COM," Sophia had smiled when she returned from her lengthy lunch. She had loved the afternoon hours spent with Stone and loved bedding him just as much. That was unusual, Sophia remarked to herself. Although she prided herself on her freedom from "catholic sophistry" and its imposition of chastity vows upon the unwed, she rarely slept with a man on the first date. Stone had been different. Stone *was* different. It was a difference Sophia intended to explore fully.

The ringing of DiGrazia's line called a halt to Sophia's private thoughts. "It's DelRay," Sophia, back at her professional duties, announced. "Should I put him off?"

DiGrazia despised talking with the chief. But this now was his responsibility. He had to get the chief to ignore the SMF. He answered Sophia's question by picking up his phone. "Chief? Any news?"

DelRay plunged into his self-aggrandizing babble. The SMF sympathizer they had arrested turned out to have had no connections, formal or informal, with the group since 1977. It was a washout for the police—and, DiGrazia suspected, for the innocent man who likely passed many hours absorbing crunching blows from police truncheons before his genuine ignorance about recent SMF-sponsored actions was established to DelRay's satisfaction.

DiGrazia spontaneously waded into a lie. He should have checked with Stone and S-COM first, he was sure, but in desperate fear that DelRay's forces would soon commit a far more damaging blunder, DiGrazia dove in. "Chief, I have news myself. Talked with the kidnappers today. Oh, yes, they were brutal. Insulting, mean, rotten, thugs. You're right. Funny thing, though . . ."—DiGrazia groped for the properly poisoned bait to toss out—"the voices in the background . . . they were speaking Sicilian, not Italian. Could this be a Mafia job?"

DelRay trembled at the suspicion. Commies he could handle. His forces had been given carte blanche to deal with them as he saw fit. Anything goes with commies, he had instructed his men, and that accorded with the charge the mayor had issued. But the Mafia? That was a different bowl of pasta. Much different. DelRay was not about to discard his police sinecure over a rich girl. If the Mafia wanted to hold her for ransom, it sat fine with DelRay. It could even mean a little extra for him at Christmas when the families came across with their bonuses, he calculated. But right now, it meant nothing to him. "Are you absolutely sure, Mr. DiGrazia? You have been under a severe strain and perhaps you misheard."

"Chief!" DiGrazia played his sizzlingly indignant role to the hilt. "I am not a tourist. I *know* Italian . . . and I know Sicilian."

"Yes, Mr. DiGrazia. I'm sure. Just checking. That's my job. Could you make out what they were saying?"

"No. I'm not fluent in Sicilian. I know just a smattering, enough to get by when forced."

"Good enough, Mr. DiGrazia. That's excellent." DelRay sincerely meant it. DiGrazia's vagueness, DelRay breathed a sigh of relief, relieved him of the obligation to pursue the angle vigorously. Meanwhile, DelRay could keep his men busy arresting campus rabble-rousers—it won the chief good press coverage. The Mafia connection would be ignored.

But, DelRay thought to himself, let's hope it is the Mafia. They are businessmen, not Marxist zealots. DiGrazia forks over the ransom; they'll return the girl—a nice, tidy deal. The press will be happy. So will the Mafia and DiGrazia. There would be no losers. Might even arrange with a few friends in the Black Hand for DelRay himself to personally discover the girl—after the money is paid, of course. Yes, DelRay thought with a smile, this DiGrazia case is looking up. He no longer felt the heat.

"Let me stress this, Mr. DiGrazia: If you get a second call, contact me promptly. Don't worry if you have to make a large ransom payment. If you decide to do it—and we have no official policy on that, although, off the record, I strongly suggest giving it serious consideration—my men will be available to you at a moment's notice. They will shadow you all the way to the drop. No sense taking chances with cash. But that's up to you to decide, Mr. DiGrazia. It is always so difficult. . . ."

DiGrazia tuned out the continuing hum of DelRay's words. Caught in the chief's flowing stream of platitudes or not, DiGrazia was happy. He recognized that the bait had been swallowed. The chief had neutralized himself. There would be no more trouble from that quarter. The Chief clearly wanted no part of this kidnapping, not anymore.

"Who are you going to believe? Me or the rich bitch?" Teresio bellowed. Gina's challenge angered him and, what's more, his testicles still ached from the squeeze Maria had given them. "I mean, get serious, Gina. 'Beware of internal dissension. It can undo a revolutionary movement faster than capitalism can,' Mao said." Teresio smiled inwardly at that one. Mao never said anything of the kind. He trusted that Gina, in her anger, would pass over it.

"Internal dissension my ass, Vincent. By your actions you've proved who the lying capitalist is: You! Twice you've tried to rape the girl. What's more, you blew it," Gina rubbed his failures in. "The big, tough revolutionary. Can't even handle a scared little rich girl."

"I can handle you, Gina," Teresio softly hissed. He could. The AK-47 in his hands ensured it. "Believe what you want, Gina. I don't care. But I am *not* taking your shit." The thrust of the gun barrel caught her in the ribs, just below her left breast. The jolt stung her. She could barely breathe; pain exploded in her chest when she tried.

"I'm out of it. That's it," Gina gasped. "Out of this stupid kidnapping and out of the SMF."

Teresio laughed. His laughter echoed through the barren hideout. It made no sense, Gina thought. He's insane. He has to be.

"Right, Gina. You're out. Just like that. *No* you're not. You're stupid, that's what. I'm going to let you walk out of here, just stroll up the street without a care in the world like a kid on the first day of school? Let you wash your hands of all *this?"* Teresio underlined his "this" by pointing the gun toward Maria's closet-cell. "I'm going to do that. *And* the pope is going to blow me. He's going to do that before an audience of one hundred thousand pilgrims to the Vatican. Do you get it, Gina? Do you?" Teresio laughed again. Harder and louder.

Gina did not get it. The searing sensations that swept through her chest had clouded her mind.

Teresio made it clear for her. "You get out of this when I've gotten the ransom money, Gina. Not before. Afterwards, I don't give a fuck what you do. You've become a nag, like an old Italian housewife. Do what you want then, but once that cunt Maria starts yapping to the police, every cop in Italy will be looking for you. But that's your problem."

In fact, it was not. Not according to Teresio's instant revision of his plan: Come Friday he would be fifty million dollars wealthier, and Gina would join Maria in dying. They were both potential witnesses now. Yes, he decided, he would hold Gina here until then. Who knows, he thought, I may need her yet. The dumb bitch. What the hell, Teresio joked to himself, he'd tie them both up and rape one, and then the other, before filling them with

AK-47 slugs. That, Teresio concluded, is what's known as having the last laugh and having it best.

"Hey, nigger! Get your black ass out of Turin." Luigi Puzo prided himself on his ability to spot a cop and applauded himself every bit as much for his skills in getting rid of cops. The lone black at the hotel bar, he has got to be fuzz, Puzo told himself. He smelled like one.

"Dirt in your ears, nigger? Answer when I talk to you!" No sweat, Puzo figured; bounce the black against the floor a few times for fun tonight, and tomorrow, Chief DelRay would have any beefs that arose straightened out. The *capo* in the Costello family, Puzo looked forward to this rumble. Since moving up the ranks, he had not enjoyed many chances to employ his own muscles. He'd use them on this black.

Myles ignored the tauts. He could not sleep in hotel beds, never had gotten a good night's rest on the road. It did not matter: He remained alert, despite a chronic lack of sleep, because if he did not he would be dead. Myles nursed his vodka tonic and wondered when the fat man in the black silk suit would get bored with his own voice. Just another drunk. Myles had heard them all, heard all they had to say.

Puzo lurched toward Myles. He was in that twilight drunk state where he perceived all his powers merging into an unbeatable force. He felt he could beat the world. But he would settle for beating "this insolent nigger."

"Fookin' wogs!" The sound cleaved the growing tension in the bar. "Goddamn fookin' greasy wogs!" Myles did not have to look over his shoulder to see what was coming. He knew.

Puzo did not.

"You calling my friend a nigger, are you? Wog! You got a big, fookin' mouth, greaseball."

That's odd, Myles observed silently. Racist Rod. The one S-COM member who never let up on the race comments and jokes, who still—even after years together in S-COM and before that in Nam—could not accept Myles's color and simply forget it. Myles knew there had been no cataclysms in Rod's tolerance. Not likely. More likely, a pint of Scotch explained Rod's rush to defend Myles. Rod always itched for a brawl, and everyone in S-COM knew that booze exacerbated his urges to fight.

Puzo, unlike Myles, did not know this. Nor did he see anything funny in this unexpected turn of events. Instead of squaring off with a lean black, he found himself looking directly in the reddening eyes of some goddamn foreigner wearing a fucking cowboy hat. That's what Puzo saw. But he was a *capo;* he could not let this lack of respect pass by.

Wordlessly, Puzo shifted his balance and called upon every ounce of strength that night's liters of vino provided. His fist flew at Rod's nose. It connected. Not with Rod's nose, but with his cheek. Puzo's aim was off.

Myles shuddered at what was about to happen. But he was damned if he was going to try to stop it and doubted if he could anyway.

A knee crashed into Puzo's groin. Stars—entire constellations—flashed before his eyes, and when he doubled over and gasped for breath, a knee to his face sent him back upwards. "Fookin' slime pot hit me in the face," Rod screamed to no one in particular. He savagely grabbed the roll of pennies from his coat pocket and smashed Puzo in the mouth. The sound of fracturing teeth mixed with that of coins falling to the floor. Puzo's blood oozed out of his lacerated mouth and his flattened nose. Myles heard him slumping to the floor. The sound of a chair breaking over Puzo's prone body capped the fight.

"Fookin' wogs. You're no better than niggers," Rod spat as he stomped out of the bar.

Myles swiveled to survey the damages. He had to commend Rod. There was no disputing the Australian's formidable skills in hand-to-hand combat. The man ceaselessly kept coming at a foe. Hit him—as Myles had witnessed desperate Viet Cong try after their ammunition was depleted—and Rod only seemed to get madder. Controlling that brutality, keeping a rein on its more psychotically vicious moments, that was the trick. It was a job only Stone could handle.

Myles downed the dregs of his drink. "Here's two

bills," he said and slid two crisp one hundred–dollar notes over to the bar man. "It should cover our expenses." Myles pointed to the splintered chair, rose from the bar, and amiably stepped over Puzo's unconscious and bleeding form.

It would be morning before Stone learned of Rod's brawl. He would not reprimand him. The man had insulted Myles and compounded his folly by slugging Rod. Stone could not—and his temperament would not—let him play nursemaid to every macho bar tough who thought he could beat the world and instead wound up getting decked by an S-COMer.

But those thoughts would play through Stone's head tomorrow, not tonight as he worked alone in his room and remained oblivious to the downstair's excitement. For now, the film alone occupied him. His portable darkroom was set up in the hotel bathroom; its trays, chemicals, and red lights sprawled across the sink and into the tub. Stone did not notice the spreading mess. He concentrated only on the film. Every inch, every frame absorbed him. He could make out the guns, AK-47s as he expected. Most terrorists turned to Russia for their armory, and this crew had not departed from Ivan's fold. A man and a woman team, that fact emerged under Stone's enhancement techniques. He wondered if they were comrades . . . or lovers. That last thought sent Stone deeper into the reels; the touch of guilt he retained over his afternoon sex with Sophia urged him to burrow into his work. Perhaps James Bond could thoroughly enjoy his on-the-job sex, but Stone was different. He was real.

Details, Stone emphasized to S-COM, details are what spell the difference between winning and losing in the field. Even if it looks insignificant now, file it away—no matter what it is. At any moment, the puzzle could unexpectedly plop into place, and that long-ago filed piece could be the missing element that would complete the design. That's why Stone studied everything his sensitive chemicals and delicate lights managed to prod out of DiGrazia's grainy film. He memorized the kidnappers' body builds, and especially admired the T-shirt-wearing girl's. He tried to glimpse their hands, their texture—maybe a look at a blemish. But the film resisted. It would yield no more.

Stone gave up and put his equipment away. It was late, long after midnight, but Stone had accomplished his mission and had squeezed out all the film had to offer. Now it was up to other sources to put S-COM smack on the kidnappers' trail. That was a road Stone yearned to walk.

CHAPTER 8

The call awakened Leah early. Seven A.M., her clock said. But the hour did not annoy her. She knew it was Thursday, and Friday marked the end of Maria DiGrazia's countdown.

"Leah, it's Dick Konvitz."

"Don't you ever sleep," Leah kidded.

"Only when the terrorists do."

That was Dick, Leah reminisced. The man seemingly never slept, never ate, never did anything but pore through accumulating files and run the agents who kept him versed in the history, philosophy, and modus operandi of every violent group. But those habits of Konvitz's that would have infuriated a wife were the very ones that made him invaluable to his government. And to S-COM.

"News, Leah. On your friends in the SMF. I've turned up two possible addresses. They're both old and I can't vouch for their current accuracy, but the informant who provided them was top-drawer. I have a bonus, too. Remember I mentioned a Teresio character?"

How could Leah forget? A probable psychotic, she had marked him down as. But that off-hand psychiatric judgment did not diminish in the slightest Teresio's potential for orchestrating a kidnapping.

"I found a picture of him, a photograph from an old University of Turin newspaper account of the SMF on campus. This Teresio, he seemed to be a SMF hanger-on at the time, but I guess he smiled nicely and the photographer used his mug to illustrate the story. There's another photograph, too—of SMF members at a campus demo. I'll toss that into the package if you like."

"Great, great! How can I thank you, Dick?"

"You can buy me lunch sometime, Leah," Konvitz shrugged off the suggestion of repayment.

"Dick, if there's ever a time you're free for lunch, I'll buy you a whole restaurant if those leads pan out. But, knowing you, you'll be tied up at work for the next twenty years. What do you do, use intravenous units?"

"My secret, Leah," Konvitz said, laughing. He appreciated Leah's compliments. She ranked as a top-notch spook in his book, even if the government had drummed her out of the service; but he knew the story behind that dismissal and maybe his cooperation was Konvitz's way of trying to compensate for that injustice. "There are *some* secrets I can keep from you."

Leah's laugh was hearty, both because of Konvitz's joke and in relief that at last S-COM was amassing leads worth pursuing. "I'll be right over to pick up the goodies, Dick. And thanks."

Stone greeted Leah's intelligence like a man breaking a two-week fast: He greedily and instantly gobbled it up and then rapidly digested it. "Leah, you keep plugging away at Konvitz and dig up whatever other loose ends can be found at the local spy shops. Lucky, head out to the Mussolini Federation. Rod, no, Myles, you look into the Costello family." It was just an intuition, a vague feeling that Stone had about the man Rod thrashed last night. It was enough to make him depart from his first thought and put Myles on the Costello angle. "Rod'll scout the SMF. I'll head over to Especiale and poke around more. We'll regroup at 1200 hours, compare notes, and get afternoon assignments. Keep the warfare to a minimum"—Stone's eyes caught Rod's: "This is not our town, our nation, or even our continent. Get tossed in jail in Turin and, if DiGrazia's portrait of Chief DelRay is even half right, you could be there until the Second Coming. Be cool. Very cool."

When the troops departed, Stone headed out to the

Especiale DiGrazia had lent him. "A needle in the haystack approach, that's what we're using," Stone cursed. With that complaint uppermost in his mind, he began to wind his Especiale through Turin's narrow roads—and hoped that DiGrazia at least had received a letter from Maria, the one he demanded from the kidnapper. Stone would then know there *was* a needle somewhere in the haystack. Somewhere.

Lucky, meantime, pursued his search for the needle at the Mussolini Federation. He knew what to look for at the Brown Shirts headquarters: telltale signs of nervousness, an explosive edginess in response to the most innocuous questions. Zip, that's what he got. Zip, too, is what Lucky thought of the Fascist group.

Myles did not hold a higher opinion of the Costello family. But, it turned out, their opinion of him was in kind.

"Holy shit, it's the nigger with a ruby for a front tooth—the one Luigi moaned about when we picked him up last night." Those words greeted Myles when he strolled into Luigi's Ristorante. The remark perversely pleased him. Myles was glad they noticed the gleaming red stone he had used instead of a conventional denture to fill in the hole where an upper front tooth had been knocked out in a boyhood street fight in the Bronx.

First, the thought hit him: The sentry in masquerade as a waiter had recognized him. Like they were looking for *him,* Myles Benet. The rest of the equation popped into Myles's mind: the drunken fat man and Rod.

"Very nice place you have here," Myles said in his fluent French.

Then the tire iron slammed into his back. Myles did not resist its force. He slid forward with it until he regained his wind and his nimble balance.

"On second thought, I don't want to eat Italian for breakfast today," he said and smiled. "Maybe tomorrow, eh?"

"Nigger, you gotta have respect. We are gonna teach it to you—no matter what it takes to pound something into your dumb-ass thick skull."

"If you insist, I'll stay. Is the food good?"

"Gripes, I heard they were stupid, but this is ridiculous."

Myles knew exactly what he was saying. And doing. His inanities slowed up his foes. Nonsense bought time; not much, but enough to measure the opposition and its strengths. Three button men, that's what he saw. Middle-aged Mafiosi who sported paunches but had arms that bulged from countless beatings of helpless victims.

Myles was far from helpless.

"You say the food's ridiculous? Too bad. I rather look forward to a tasty breakfast. Guess I'll have to cancel my reservation."

"Nigger, you got it wrong. You made it easy for us, coming here. Because of you, our *capo* is in the hospital. We're gonna put you in your grave."

The three hulking men converged on Myles. The little one carried the tire iron; he twirled it like a majorette handles her baton. The other two carried knives. Long blades. But they were no knife fighters, Myles could tell. They stomped forward toward him on flat feet.

"So sorry, but I don't think you'll make the dance company," Myles giggled. He nearly laughed. This, he told himself, is an absurdly bad bet. Three against one. The odds were just too much in Myles's favor.

"What a dreadful mistake. I was looking for the Welcome Wagon, and you know, I don't think this is the place. No way to treat a newcomer to Turin, I might add." While he talked, Myles's left hand darted into a pocket and retrieved a blade. A keepsake from his days on the streets of the Bronx, the switchblade had accompanied Myles to Nam and everywhere since. A nudge of the button and the five-inch blade emerged with a click.

Myles balanced himself on his toes. He gracefully tossed the open blade from one hand to the other and, in another habit that dated from the Bronx, muttered a stream of street-Spanish curses. "Su madre es la puta, marica!" "Your mother is a whore, faggot!" That old incantation amused him, helped to pass the time to the moment of the strike.

Myles's right hand flew out and grabbed the end of the

tire iron. In a seemingly continuous motion, the left hand slashed the knife deep and broad along the little man's face. "Touché, I'd say." He would live but, by Myles instant calculation, would be wearing forty-eight stitches from his eye, down the cheek, through one nostril, and over both eyes. Myles slammed the tire iron into the man's forehead and put him out cold.

"I must've bored the poor little guy to sleep. I know it. I'm such a beastly bore," Myles quipped as he discarded the tire iron and turned his attention full on the other two Mafiosi. They were slow, horribly slow, Myles knew. There had been a split second, the moment when he swung the iron, that he left himself wide open for a knife in the ribs. He had bet they would not realize this, and as usual, Myles collected the bet.

Another quick flick and Myles's knife poked between the lower ribs of his closer attacker. Moving the knife horizontally, Myles sliced through several inches of the man's lower chest, turned the blade sharply downwards, and withdrew it from what remained of the man's lacerated stomach.

The move had taken too long, Myles sensed. Superb as his skills with a knife remained, they had been better when street life in the Bronx provided nearly daily practice. To survive, it took a knife or a gun, and Myles had opted for the blade; it felt more comfortable in his hand, more a part of his lithe body than did a gun. When the choice presented itself, Myles's diamond-studded .32 caliber pistol stayed in his pocket.

But Myles was right about the time. He saw the knife coming at him as he rushed to tug his own knife out of the second man's belly. The fastest man Myles had saved for last, and now the man struck. His stiletto scraped along the leather jacket Myles invariably wore when on duty—precisely because the tough hide successfully deflected blades. Then the man's stiletto slid into Myles's hand, cutting as it moved along the skin, and bared the hand down to the bone. But Myles let the man keep at it. A hand wound never killed anyone.

A stomach wound did, if the man who inflicted it knew how and where to cut. Myles's blade plunged deep into his last attacker's wide-open stomach. In anger he later rebuked himself for—Myles loathed anger; he knew it robbed a fighter of the rational edge that could spell the margin between living or dying—Myles deliberately and methodically cut a figure-eight inside the man. When he removed his knife, the man's small intestine—inch after inch after inch—began to unravel and plop, plop, plop it slid to the floor with a ghostly splat.

"No thank you. No intestines for me today," Myles commented as he studied his morning's work. "But it *is* a real nice place you have here, I want you to know."

Triage, Myles thought. He remembered the term from a book he had read on World War I, when makeshift and harried field hospitals classified incoming wounded into three groups: Those who were sure to live; those who likely would live if they received immediate medical attention; and those who would die, no matter what efforts the staff expended. The practice of dividing the wounded into those three groups—playing God, if you will—is what triage is.

Myles recognized he had performed triage of a different, more gristly sort: He observed the sure corpse whose innards lay strewn on the bloody floor, the maybe, and the little man who would live. No sense finishing the other two off, Myles decided. The Costello family, he had concluded, would be "out of its league even in a nickel-and-dime operation like the DiGrazia kidnapping," as he later reported to Stone. Besides, Myles could not stomach cutting a man when he was down. That was more to Rod's liking.

"Except I'd change the name. Luigi's is so common. I got it: How about calling this place the Triage Café," Myles quipped as he exited.

Rod, of all the S-COM scouts, encountered the most bewilderment on his mission. Rod could take orders; he thrived on brutal fights and violence; he backed down from no man; he could figure out how to assemble and take down any gun ever made. But he hated mysteries—and that was what he found in his quest for the SMF.

With Konvitz's pair of addresses in hand, Rod briskly

headed to the nearer of the two. He could walk to that one, and in foreign lands, he could never bring himself to trust taxi drivers. The more distant address, the second one, he would put off until he had poked around this closer site.

Rod stared at the building. He saw an abandoned shell, that was all. "A fookin' bomb ripped through the joint long ago," Rod thought aloud. "It's home to nothing but rats now."

Boarded-up windows prevented a look inside. A ramshackle staircase deterred Rod from a walk upstairs to poke about. He could see his 190 pounds tumbling through the rotten wood and hear the jokes that Myles and Lucky would laugh at his expense when, hours later, a worried Stone commissioned a search party to locate the missing Rod. No, Rod would take on a platoon of fifteen heavily armed men if Stone ordered him to, but he would not risk the humiliation that would follow a fall through those rotten boards. Besides, his ears detected nothing. Not a single sound from above.

Rod knew better than to depart this address so soon, however. He started to canvass passers-by, storekeepers, anyone he could corner and whom he could make understand his Australian-accented English. "SMF? The Seventh Mao Force? Have you heard of 'em lately? Seen 'em? Noticed any activity in this building? Any people going in or out?" Rod continued the litany of questions long into the morning. But even the few Italians who could comprehend Rod's questions offered no information. They had heard of the SMF, sure—*everyone* in Turin had. But, no, there had been no signs, no indications whatsoever of the SMF in the neighborhood. Not in several years.

It was a hopeless search. Rod glanced at his watch and, with relief, saw that 1200 hours was nearing. He headed back to the noon rendezvous with Stone and S-COM, bringing a report that consisted of a string of nothings. The damn group had vanished. Maybe, Rod hoped, they would be at the second address. But with the noon hour fast approaching, a look at that site had to wait.

"Goddamit!" Teresio complained when one of his frequent and nervous glances out of a crack in his hide-out's boarded-up windows turned up a sight of a man in a cowboy hat snooping around. But Teresio could not figure this one. The man obviously was not a cop—no Italian strolled the streets in an outfit like that. A private detective? Not likely, Teresio calculated. *Nobody* would hire someone who looked that foolish. Perhaps it was a prospective purchaser, a field representative from an Australian company. That made sense—sort of, Teresio supposed. But it did not make complete sense, and Teresio continued to puzzle over the man and his mission as the fellow walked up and down the street and engaged everyone in conversation. It *must* be a private dick, Teresio thought. But who would hire such a ludicrous character? Not DiGrazia. It would not be DiGrazia's style to employ someone that conspicuously odd. DiGrazia prized beauty and style—why else did he make Especiales?

Teresio would have mulled longer on the man's identity and purpose, but it was Thursday and his own schedule got more hectic as Maria's calendar counted down. And now he was going it alone.

Gina, he decided when he awoke that morning, posed too much of an unpredictable risk. Her mouth just never stopped. He had debated whether he should plug her there and then; set the AK-47 on rock n' roll and let the bullets put an end to her stupid whining mouth and the troubles it could cause. But the roaring noise of the bullets could bring trouble—and it would arrive immediately. Someone, some doddering biddy, Teresio was sure, would call the cops. They might even investigate, and if they did, it would mean trouble.

Troubles Teresio did not need now. He had plenty. After making up his mind about Gina, there had been but a single solution: Tie her up, gag her mouth, and toss her in the closet with the DiGrazia girl. They deserved each other, Teresio believed.

But that meant he now had to do every job, take every little step on his own. He had dictated the innocuous note to Maria; she had compliantly written down his string of revolutionary slogans; and the letter had already been posted to DiGrazia. He'd even had to steal food for himself—screw the girls; they could starve for all he cared. And now he had to leave the hide-out again, this time to call DiGrazia with the final ransom instructions. He had no choice. Gina and the DiGrazia girl had to be left here alone. There was no other way.

Before going he double-checked the lock on the closet door. It was secure. A good Yale lock, he had robbed it himself. It would hold them in.

Maria heard Teresio's rumbling about the outside room, and then she heard him leaving the hide-out and bolting the outside lock. When he dumped Gina into her cell that morning, Maria had been confused, but that was par for this course. She had tried to talk with Gina, to find out what the nut was doing now, but Gina's rapid head-shakes told her to keep quiet. Maria had obeyed the mute order. Gina, she knew, would tell her when it was safe to talk.

Strange, Maria thought to herself in the first moments after Teresio exited the hide-out. Peculiar. He gags Gina, but not me. He had remembered to bind her hands and feet, but in his anxious haste, he neglected the final touch.

Maria silently inched herself closer to Gina. Just to be near her. Somehow the closeness made her feel more secure. If only she could ungag Gina, she could find out about this new twist in an increasingly bizarre mystery. She moved her mouth up as if to kiss Gina on the lips. With her teeth, she gripped Gina's carelessly knotted gag and slowly, carefully, inched it downward.

"Guess I'm in the same boat," Gina calmly said when at last she could talk. "Maria, you don't know how sorry I am. About all of this." Gina sobbed; just tiny tears, but they were big enough to let Maria glimpse the dangers, the mutual perils that awaited them both.

"He's going to kill us, isn't he?"

"I think so. I don't know. Probably."

"Up until this morning when he locked you up, too, I thought I'd live. I thought Papa would pay him and I'd be home. It was bad, but I could stand it—I had to stand it—until I got freed. But now . . ." Maria joined Gina in crying the dry, horrified tears that people cry when they are at the end of the line and know it.

"Is there anything, anything at all that we can do, Gina? There must be. There has to be."

"Wait. That's all. Just wait. Hope the police—" Gina had to snicker at the improbability of the idea, "hope they find us. Hope your father has hired private detectives who free us. Hope that Vincent makes another mistake, a big one. Just hope, Maria."

To pound thoughts of their impending executions out of their minds, the girls talked of their pasts, their futures, and avoided all mention of the dismal present. School, old boyfriends, dimly remembered priests from their childhoods filled their conversation. Maria spoke of cars; her love for them and of her love for Especiales in particular. She talked of her father's business, his generosity, his gentle kindness. She confided that she doubted he could raise $50 million or anything close.

Gina had already figured that. Teresio, as usual, had overshot. If the cash had been in reach, Gina suspected DiGrazia would have anted up days ago. But $50 million was unprecedented. Most kidnappers, even in inflation-ridden Italy, demanded one million, maybe two or three million dollars. Nobody had ever asked for $50 million; certainly no kidnapper had ever gotten so much.

"Papa will work something out. I know it," Maria insisted. Her insistence was hollow. Neither woman believed it; not completely.

Then Gina confessed her fears. Even if somehow they were rescued, her life was still over. Kidnapping—Gina did not mention or allow herself to think about her passive roles in the post office explosion and the Albanese murders—is a major felony. Years and years in dirty, vicious jails jammed tight with lesbians and with jailors who raped female prisoners at will. It was not a pretty picture Gina sketched.

"Papa will work something out there, too," Maria consoled. And he just might, Maria thought—or, maybe, she might herself.

But such long-distance reflections, both girls realized, were academic anyway. Anything past Friday might as well have been in the thirty-eighth century or beyond. It was the stuff of fairy tales and fantasies.

"You got the cash, pig?"

"Nearly all of it," DiGrazia lied into his telephone as Stone nodded his approval. "By tomorrow, I'll have every last lira, all fifty million worth."

"And you got the letter from your kid?"

"Yes." The letter would have pained DiGrazia under different circumstances. It attacked him and Especiale for brutalizing workers, destroying Turin, and down the list of standard leftist grievances. It evinced no imagination in its construction, Stone had observed—just commie pap heisted from Mao's *Little Red Book*. Both DiGrazia and Stone had known at a glance that Maria's hand had been used to communicate another's message. But the letter served its purpose. It proved to Stone's satisfaction and to DiGrazia's unmitigated joy that Maria was still alive. At least she was yesterday, when the letter was written and, Stone hazarded a hunch, probably still was since there had been no apparent changes in the kidnappers' situation.

"Put the money—small bills, remember that asshole—in suitcases. Deliver the suitcase to the address I gave you. Come alone. You will be watched all the way. If there is a hint of a tail, of police surveillance, your daughter dies. Got it?"

DiGrazia understood, and he recognized the drop-off site for the ransom as near the University of Turin campus.

"This is my final communication with you, fucker. Make sure you understand every instruction. And make sure you do them right. There must be *no* deviations."

"But, wait!" DiGrazia interrupted the caller before he hung up. "What about Maria? Where do I pick her up?"

The question threw Teresio. He had not considered it; there was no need to. "Shithead! Cocksucking capitalist!" It enraged him that DiGrazia dared to ask questions. "She'll be in touch with you," he spat and abruptly hung up the phone.

Stone did not share with DiGrazia all the deductions he drew from the kidnapper's call. He simply complimented DiGrazia on doing his job superbly, predicted that all would be well, and walked away to find the solitude he needed to sift through his gelling ideas.

The kidnapper was a rank amateur, that was obvious. No professional would demand $50 million in small bills in suitcases—not unless he had a small army to cart away the dozens of cases that would be required to hold a mountain of cash. A group that mustered only two people to execute the DiGrazia kidnapping did not have an army at its disposal. The man, clearly, had no idea how much money, how much paper, was involved in a transaction of this magnitude. That ruled out the Costello family. Has-been dope dealers they may be, but Stone was confident they could comprehend the size of a fifty million–dollar pile of bills. The Mussolini Federation, Stone conceded, remained a possibility. But a remote one. The selection of a drop near the university pointed at the SMF. Again, the amateurism, the ignorance about cash, the fondness for colleges: All the fingers pointed straight at the Seventh Mao Force.

Nor did Stone share a darker deduction with DiGrazia. The terrorist's angry hesitation and vagueness about Maria's reunion with her father pointed to only one conclusion: There would be no release. In a sense, that made Stone's job simpler. He need not fret that perhaps he had steered DiGrazia the wrong way when he should have been urging him to somehow pay off the kidnapper. But it made Stone's job harder, too. There would be no relief in the countdown—Maria's life was fast expiring.

"Stone?" Sophia interrupted his gloomy deductions. He welcomed her, and she enjoyed his glance at her enticing body. "There's a call for you. Police Chief DelRay. He demands to talk to you immediately. Stone, he sounds angry. I just wanted you to be prepared." Stone shrugged and lifted the receiver.

"Where do you and your bully-boys get off, Williams? What the hell do you think you're doing? First off, you have no damn business in Turin—"

"Hold it, Chief. I am in the employ of Mr. Salvatore DiGrazia. That explains my business."

But DelRay was not to be placated so simply. Not this morning and not after he received an earlier call from Luigi Puzo. Puzo was mad, and *that* made DelRay mad. "It does not, Williams. Not at all. Your man, that Australian, last night he mercilessly and without provocation assaulted a Turin citizen and respectable businessman. This morning another of your men, the Negro with the ruby tooth, invades Luigi's Ristorante and kills one man, puts another in intensive care, and permanently scars the face of a third. Again, without a shred of provocation. Williams, I'm putting the lot of you under arrest."

Shit, Stone muttered. It was the first he knew of Myles's knife play. But he trusted Myles's judgment, and he already knew everything he needed to know about DelRay's. Stone would have relished telling DelRay to shove his stupidities where the moon don't shine, but he stifled the urge. He could not afford a night in jail, not with Maria DiGrazia's life hanging in a precarious balance.

"Chief, there's no need to be precipitous and no need to arrest anyone. Look, I'll be down to see you in the station house. I'll explain it all, and Mr. DiGrazia, I'm sure, will back me up on this one hundred percent. *He* will vouch for my behavior and intentions." DelRay, Stone reckoned, might go *mano a mano* against an American outsider but DiGrazia was a significant member of the community; he would be a different and unignorable matter. Stone reckoned right.

"I will be waiting for you, Mr. Williams," DelRay oozed into his telephone. Stone caught the meaning. Extraordinary expenses would be involved, after all. Ten thousand dollars will buy off a penny-ante police chief, Stone calculated. To be safe, however, he asked DiGrazia for $20,000. Just in case.

Stone picked up the tail immediately upon leaving the Especiale offices. It did not stand to be DelRay's cops. Nor were the dark-suited men from the SMF. They were too old, and they did their work too well. Stone admitted they were pretty good at keeping him within sight without piling right on top of him. They gave him line, the way a patient fisherman plays out a trout before reeling the fish in. Stone patted the twenty grand in his wallet and started to take in the local attractions, like a tourist on a tranquil morning jaunt. He was in no hurry. When they wanted to pull in their catch, Stone would feel the tug on the line. He was sure of it.

The morning sun shone. It was a beautiful day in Turin. Stone breathed in its peacefulness; soon the streets would bustle with laborers, secretaries, and executives on lunch breaks. But now the city stood becalmed.

A harsh noise echoed through the stillness. Stone recognized it instantly for the tug on his line. Some would have mistook the shattering sound for a firecracker or an exhaust backfire, since that is what a .22-caliber shot sounds like. The men were indeed professionals, Stone computed. Pros prefer the tiny noise of a .22 and the way it blends into the cacophony of sounds every city holds. But they were rusty at their trade. The shot had been fired too soon. It missed Stone.

Stone dove between parked cars. The tails had split up; he saw one peeling off to the left as he unholstered his 9 mm automatic. Stone unhurriedly squeezed off five shots at the moving form and saw the man collapse motionless to the street. One down; one to go. Stone complimented Leah for her borrowed HK automatic pistol—thirteen shots remained in the magazine.

Stone aimed his attention at the remaining man. The man had followed Stone's lead and had ducked between parked cars. A Fiat 128, a Renault, and another Fiat separated the combatants. Stone could see the man's swarthy face; he was sweating from the exertion. In his fifties and bedecked in a dark suit, dark shirt, and a yellow tie, the man could have stepped out of any Hollywood movie on the Mafia; he was that much of a caricature. Stone laughed.

Stone could see the man's eyes concentrating on him, trying to figure out what the next move should be. Stone was doing the same. But the blur his peripheral vision detected preempted the right of either Stone or the man to choose.

The man's gun flew to the sidewalk. A knee, knee, right to the face combination exploded all over him. "Thanks, Rod," Stone shouted over the cars.

"Anytime, boss."

In shocked horror, Stone numbly witnessed Rod's next move. It was too late to stop it, and truth is, Stone did not choose to try. Turin and its tensions had worn thin. Even so, Stone averted his sight from Rod; there were times when Rod's passion for hand-to-hand combat got more than a little *out* of hand. This was one of those times.

Rod had draped the unconscious man's mouth over the curb; his lips and teeth kissed the hard concrete. Then, to a steady chorus of "Fookin' wogs!" Rod jumped with both feet on the man's head. Again and again. And once again. The man's face, what was left of it, melted into the curb under the force generated by Rod's powerful stomps. There were no teeth to be seen in the man's mouth when Rod concluded his business; there was only blood.

"Fookin' wogs will never learn, the smelly slime pots," Rod merrily declared when he joined Stone. "Well, we left that one with something to chew on: bloody Chiclets," Rod guffawed at his own joke.

Stone glanced at Rod's boots. Blood saturated them. Fresh blood from the hole where the man's mouth had been. He grimaced. But he knew Rod had done his job, that's all. Rod played by the war rules. Stone rebuked him only when Rod's zeal for blood swept in bystanders. But Rod could finish fights that others started any way he chose. Those were the only rules Rod knew, and Stone was not about to change that.

"You want my report now . . . or back at the hotel, Stone?"

"Later, Rod. You head back there now. Tell the others to have lunch. I'll be awhile."

"Yes, sir!" Rod barked and trotted off. Stone had to smile at the retreating figure of good old, maniacal Rod and the wonderful fighting machine he was. But now Stone had another death—and one more beating—to explain away in DelRay's office. He was glad he had taken $20,000.

"Good to meet you, Chief," Stone said, grinning thinly when he arrived at the police station and had entered DelRay's office. Stone hated the politicking his leadership role thrust upon him, but it had to be done; and Stone, like it or not, did it—and did it well.

"Understand there was some trouble on your way over here?" DelRay returned Stone's smile, but more broadly.

The Chief's mood had changed; Stone could sense it. "A little, I'm afraid. We handled it ourselves. Tell me, Chief, who are these guys?"

"On the record or off?"

Stone knew with DelRay there would be no on-the-record responses worth listening to. He quickly indicated his choice by putting five one thousand–dollar bills on DelRay's desk. DelRay sealed the deal by walking to his office door and shutting it tightly. He greedily pocketed the cash when he sat down. "They are—or were—the Costello family."

"Here's five thousand more, American dollars in crisp currency, Chief. What else can you tell me?"

"Not much to tell, really. Thanks to you, Mr. Williams"—it was *Mister* Williams now, Stone noticed—"they are rapidly ceasing to be a threat to the good citizens of Turin. To be honest, Mr. Williams, they never were much here: smalltime hoodlums who staked out Turin when they were driven out of the United States. You understand, we do not—*never*—have had a Mafia problem in Turin."

"This problem that does not exist . . . The Costellos . . . Will we be seeing more of them?"

"No. I give you my word as Chief. They are no longer your worry. I can assure you."

"Good to hear that, Chief." Stone well knew that when a police chief of DelRay's ilk says "to be honest" and "I assure you," the lies were sure to flow in a flood. But Stone also knew that kind of police chief always sided with the team that had the most money and muscle. Since he represented DiGrazia's wealth and S-COM's muscle, Stone held the winning hand in DelRay's game. But Stone could not resist playing another card or two: "Here's another five thousand, Chief. That makes fifteen grand, American money. I trust the incidents of the past will be forgotten and we can be cooperative friends."

"You can count on me, Mr. Williams," DelRay said as he pocketed the last of the cash. "It *is* a pleasure."

"Pleasure doing business with you, Chief," Stone said as he departed. "Back to the DiGrazia case."

"About that, Mr. Williams. I trust that if there are, well, positive developments I will be brought in."

So that's another sweetener DelRay wants, Stone said to himself. He's betting we may—just might—happily unravel the DiGrazia knot. And if we do, he wants to grab some credit. Figures. It definitely figures.

"I promise you, Chief," Stone said in closing, "you can count on me."

He almost had to laugh at DelRay. The stupid—what is it Rod says?—*wog*. That's it. A stupid wog is what DelRay is. Stone smiled. He had not thought DelRay would fall for it; nobody would. But DelRay had splashed right in. Even after Stone explicitly mentioned money, the man had said nothing to establish a ground for doubt. He had plowed straight ahead, and Stone had the tape to prove it. It was a tape he never wanted to use, *but*—the slightest grumble from DelRay and that tape would be on the desk of Turin's biggest TV station within an hour. Insurance, that's what the tape was. The way things were going in Turin, Stone needed all the insurance he could buy. He only wished that the solution to Maria DiGrazia's kidnapping would come as easily.

Stone's high spirits sank when his gathered troops delivered reports on their morning's work. Rod's news was particularly unwelcome. Stone had already largely discounted the theory that either the Costello family or the Mussolini Federation was using the SMF banner as a mask; Lucky's account of the Brown Shirts, plus his own and Myles's encounters with the Costellos, supported him. Which left only the SMF and that one, unchecked address. It wasn't much, and Leah's latest round of the intelligence community had produced nothing more. The bone was picked clean, except for the single scrap the last address represented.

But Stone had noticed something else. A small detail. He could not remove his eyes from the photograph of the old SMF demonstration Leah had brought back from Konvitz. There was something about it. Finally, Stone's memory clicked: the girl in the DiGrazia film, the kidnapper. Stone swore he saw her in the SMF picture too. It was not enough to draw a firm conclusion; not even enough to mention. He was going by the likeness in body builds and by the striking coincidence that both women wore the same T-shirt, one with Mona Lisa silk-screened on the front. There could be a thousand girls like that in Turin, Stone knew—but he doubted it. It *was* the same girl. He would bet on it. All the chips now were on the SMF, and with Maria DiGrazia's time running out fast, Stone wanted to cover that bet in a hurry.

"We move out, troops," Stone snapped. "Full battle gear. Pack *everything*. With who knows how many Costellos out gunning for us, despite the promises of the police chief, and with nobody-can-guess how many guns in the SMF's hands, we take no chances."

Nobody argued with the order. With each S-COMer acutely aware of Maria DiGrazia's disappearing life and with Myles's bandaged hand serving as a constant reminder of the intentions of the Costello family toward S-COM, the troops itched for a fight. They all hoped the next stop provided it.

CHAPTER 9

S-COM arrived at the address in Turin's suburbs. It was an old villa, with plenty of land on all sides. The house screamed for upkeep—new paint especially—and might have belonged to an aging member of Italy's discarded nobility. That did not preclude it as an SMF hide-out: More than a few sons and daughters of former aristocrats have embraced the political extremes, and the SMF, Stone knew, could have easily been the beneficiary of such a misguided patron.

Stone took no chances. The house and its remoteness gave no clues to what lurked within. A heavily armed SMF gang could be the reception party. Or perhaps it would be an innocuous count and his countess. Stone had no way of telling—except to approach the villa. Nor could he risk entering with S-COM's guns ablaze: The victims could be that harmless count and countess whom Stone pictured sitting by their fireplace and chatting about their golden days when they and their brethren ruled Italy.

Slow and easy, that's how S-COM had to assault the house. "Do *not,*" Stone emphatically underlined the negative, "do *not* shoot until fired on." Just one rip from an S-COM Heckler and Koch MP5 machine gun would Swiss-cheese the house and likely send its inhabitants, innocent or not, to the morgue. "Spread out. Myles, take the rear of the villa. Lucky, go to the left; Rod, to the right. Leah and I have the front. Keep it peaceful. We'll try to smoke whoever is in there out from our side. But *nobody* escapes. If they come out unarmed, do not shoot. Take prisoners—alive." Stone aimed that caveat at Rod. "If the DiGrazia girl's not within and this is the SMF, they'll retaliate. She'll be dead tonight—unless we can find out where she is from someone inside. That," Stone grimaced, "can be your job, Rod." A few minutes with Rod and even Scrooge would part with his last pennies, Stone knew. No SMF member could long stand up to Rod's merciless techniques for squeezing information out of a suspect. "Head out," Stone barked.

Stone weighed his tactics. He saw three options. He mulled each in turn.

He could enter the house by stealth and, by that route, gain a look around. If the count theory panned out, he could exit just as quietly, round up his troops, and be back at the hotel without ever disturbing the occupants.

On the other hand, Stone could saunter up to the door, knock, and see what greeted him.

Lastly, S-COM could mount a diversion outside. A noise. Anything to attract the attention of those within. If they were innocent bystanders, it would be apparent. If they were not, Stone bet they would overplay their hand—and emerge firing nervously.

A student of gambling is what Stone was; not a gambler. That ruled out the knock on the door and made Stone less than eager to attempt the entry-by-stealth approach.

His best option, Stone calculated, was to goad the people inside the house into playing their hand. That meant attracting their attention.

"Leah," he whispered, "bring any of your shurikens?"

Leah responded by lifting a lethal kung fu star from her pocket.

"Break the big window." If the inhabitants are noncombatants, Stone reckoned they would strike the shattered glass up to the work of mischievous kids. A follow-up money order from "a friend" would set the financial accounts right. That is, *if* they are noncombatants.

Leah fingered the shuriken, a perfectly balanced star.

Made of steel and one-eighth of an inch thick, the shuriken weighed in at a quarter-ounce. Because of its balance and eight points, it will stick into anything it is aimed at. Or, in the case of glass, throw a shuriken correctly, and the glass splinters into hundreds of shards.

Leah did not have to take aim. Even an untrained thrower could hit the large target Stone had indicated. With a fast flick of her skilled wrist, the shuriken took off at a rapid speed—in the neighborhood of 50 miles per hour, Leah guessed. However fast the shuriken flew, it was fast enough. Glass tinkled to the ground from the big window.

Stone tensely waited. He lay on the ground, and after hurling the shuriken, Leah joined him in the dirt. Seconds passed and Stone sighed, relieved: No S-COM fighter had mistaken the sound of breaking glass for gun fire and responded with a premature burst of MP5 bullets.

A fat man with a bandage on his nose came up to the window for a look. Stone did not recognize the man, although he did recognize the style—and it definitely was not the SMF's. "More Mafia," he observed.

"Check it out," the bandaged fat man commanded from within. A trio of silk-suited men—still looking like movie extras from central casting, Stone chuckled to himself—opened the front door and cautiously surveyed the grounds. They were armed with sawed-off shotguns.

"They've hit the mattresses," Stone explained softly to Leah. "The Costellos think they're in a gang war. With us. No sense disappointing them." Stone touched the trigger of his MP5. In his book, the Costellos were bad news. An aggravating distraction from the more pressing business of saving Maria DiGrazia. That's all they were: a nuisance. But they had repeatedly asked S-COM for trouble. Stone did not want to let them down.

For a moment, he considered playing fair and casting aside his submachine gun and relying on the Mercury magnum shotgun he also packed. But Stone dismissed that idea fast. These were war rules; the Costellos had picked them. Besides, the shotguns would take too long to finish the job.

Stone squeezed the MP5 trigger. The three men in the

search party had clumped together. For safety, probably, Stone thought in the split second between the trigger squeeze and the gun's chatter. Like paper targets at a shooting range, the men tumbled—one, two, three—to the ground. Unlike paper targets, they bled: profusely and on their way to a nonnegotiable meeting with death. Stone admired the nineteen-inch weapon in his hands. Its 9 mm slugs burst into the men with unexcelled accuracy. A real beauty, this gun, Stone acknowledged as he withdrew the spent magazine and inserted another thirty rounds.

Leah's MP5, meanwhile, had taken out what was left of the big window. Sprays of bullets from the back and both sides—the work of Myles, Rod, and Lucky—joined the metallic chorus. Stone cursed the Costello family for wasting his—and Maria DiGrazia's—time, but this, he decided, is their last round in the fight. His continuing MP5 fire illustrated his determination as Stone pumped round after round into the villa.

Intermittent shotgun fire answered S-COM's bullets. Stone instructed Leah to cover the front while he carefully worked his way to Rod's position. "Join Myles in the back," Stone ordered the Australian. When they crept to Myles's position—shotgun blasts tailing their every move, but miraculously missing—Stone whispered orders to Myles, left Rod under his command, and moved out to find Lucky.

Lucky, too, was sent to the villa's rear, and Stone finally rejoined Leah. "We're going inside in two minutes," he hissed.

They filled their waiting time with more MP5 fire. Based upon the frequency and location of return shotgun fire from within, Stone had calculated the Costello strength at no more than four men. But the Costellos could keep up like this all night; their positions within the villa afforded too much protection. Stone wanted to terminate this battle and rush back to his more critical business.

When zero hour struck, Stone took the lead in charging the front door. Myles would be doing the same in the rear, Stone knew. A stray shotgun pellet creased Stone's left leg. Nothing serious; he kept moving straight ahead.

Meanwhile, Myles, Rod, and Lucky had forced their way in through the back door. "I'll be damned if it ain't the fookin' wog from the bar," Stone heard after a remorseless stream of MP5 slugs.

A mop-up operation was all that faced S-COM. Stone's estimate of four gunmen had been errant. Once there were six, but four now lay dead. Just two remained, and both were flying white flags and begging for mercy; their guns had been thrown to the ground in surrender.

"Lucky. Rod. Finish up here. Leah and Myles, we're going back to the hotel."

"But Stone," Leah protested when the departing threesome left the house. "Stone, you know there will be no prisoners."

"Do you care, Leah?" Stone, for one, did not. He had had his fill of the Costellos.

"Not if we find Maria DiGrazia alive."

"We will. That's our job."

Back in the villa, Rod and Lucky understood Stone's parting command. "Up against the wall, wogs," Rod shouted. "No, you fookin' dummies. Face me. I don't like to shoot a man in the back. Lucky, will you do the honors, my boy?"

"It's your party, Rod. I can't deprive you."

"Come on, Lucky. It's easy, laddie. Let's just make quick work of it, okay?"

"No, Rod. I'd really prefer you do it."

Lucky, Rod remembered, had not shared the Vietnam experience. The war rules did not sit well with him. He had not seen the mangled, bloody results of Viet Cong "mercy." Nor had he ever had to shoot a buddy whose wounds made it impossible for him to travel, whose wounds caused him such pain that his screams penetrated every survivor in his platoon. But there would be no medical relief for him, not in Nam's boondocks, and to leave him behind meant leaving him to be tortured by the Cong. One clean shot behind the ear put him out of pain. Rod had fired his share of those shots. They were the only shots that caused him to tremble when he squeezed them off.

"Not got the heart for it, Lucky?"

"The stomach, Rod. You know me—a lover, not a fighter."

"What the fuck are you talking about," Frankie Costello screamed. "Don't you know me? I'm a boss. I can make it worth your while."

"What about him?" Rod gestured with his gun at Costello's sweating companion.

"He's a button man, a soldier."

"You don't care, you're saying?" Rod asked.

"It's up to you," Costello said, managing a smile. "But if *I* walk out of here, there's big, big money in it for you."

"From what? Pimping, dope, loan-sharking, and the rest of your filthy business, fookin' slime pot."

"Hey, the *money's* clean," Costello protested.

It did him no good. Treachery to a comrade—that ranked as an unforgivable sin in Rod's code. Not that he would have considered letting Costello and his soldier escape. That was not his order. But the scent of betrayal made it easier for Rod to pull the trigger. He emptied the magazine; all thirty rounds pumped into the bodies, with twenty-seven reserved for Costello. "Fookin' traitorous wog. Don't even treat his own kind good."

Lucky reluctantly agreed. The man, he concurred, did not deserve to live. Nonetheless, he was glad Rod was there to handle the job. It was one he would someday have to perform for S-COM, but Lucky was in no rush. Not for that kind of job.

While Stone got his wounded leg stitched and patched —"just a flesh wound," the Especiale doctor reassured— the remaining S-COM troopers joined in the hotel bar for a fast beer and a comparing of notes. Except Leah. She had requested, and Stone had granted her permission, to take a long look at the SMF address Rod had investigated earlier that day.

"It's only a hunch, Stone," Leah admitted. "But what do we have left? It's our only possibility."

Stone had not relished the prospect of Leah prowling about a suspected terrorist hide-out in the dark, but she was right: There were no more options. Besides, Leah's skills at night surveillance-and-penetration operations were unsurpassed. Israel taught its agents well how to move, strike, and retreat using darkness as a natural ally. Leah, Stone could confidently document, had learned her lessons superbly. Nor had Stone countermanded her desire to go this alone. He knew why: She was the best at it.

So now Leah stood behind a telephone pole and stared at the suspected address. Like a *ninja* in Samurai Japan, she saw without being seen; any movement she made flowed into the darkness and remained hidden by the night from all except thoroughly trained observers.

But it took no special training or skills for Leah to instantly recognize that something was afoot in the building. A dim light flickered within the boarded-up windows. Someone, something, was inside. That was certain.

Leah's eyes surveyed the ramshackle staircase. She used no light, but as her eyes grew increasingly accustomed to the gloom, she picked a safe way up the steps. She could only hope the old and dry wood would not creak a warning sound.

Leah moved daintily, almost like a ballerina, up the rotting and wounded stairs. There were no noises, not from Leah's ascent or from within the second floor. At the door, she intently peered through the keyhole. A candle bounced its light within. There was no other motion. Just the flicker of a dying candle.

Leah gently tried the door knob. It responded with a slight groan to her pressure. She froze in the staircase and strove to become one with its blackness. She unholstered her pistol and waited.

Nobody stirred within. Leah turned the knob more forcefully. It moved, but the door showed no sign of yielding. "Locked from within," Leah observed to herself.

It did not add up. An empty room. Utter silence. Desolation.

But the candle told Leah all she needed to know.

Someone was using the room for something, that was certain. Candles do not burn forever. They must be tended to. But by whom? And how many?

Leah slipped back outside and headed toward S-COM's base. Whoever was inside and wherever they had disappeared to, Leah did not want to accidentally bump into them on the way out. She moved fast. S-COM had its work cut out.

Teresio bitterly cursed himself for coming up with what he now demeaned as a fool idea. He had been walking for forty-five minutes, maybe longer, up and down a block in the hotel district. His stomach growled; his legs ached from the miles of pacing he had logged. But still he strode back and forth. Be patient, he chided himself. A revolution is not made in a day. The opportunity will arrive.

He congratulated himself on his choice of blocks. His was a deadly dark section of street, but smack within the narrow network of avenues and alleys that lead to Turin's best hotels, the ones which house transient tourists from abroad: usually Americans, Germans, or Japanese come to Turin to tour the automobile factories.

It was just such a tourist Teresio waited for. Gina was right: He would never make a shoplifter. It made him too nervous, and in his fright, he never heeded watching eyes. Tonight of all nights, he would make no errors. He could not. Not when he sat just this side of $50 million. But his stomach uninterruptedly sent its incessant call for food. He felt like celebrating—and why not? He was about to become a very, very rich man. Literally, an overnight financial success.

He maintained his vigil for the right tourist. So far, few people had passed him, and none fulfilled his requirements. They came in groups of two or three, or in one case, a lone Japanese man had walked by. It was not that Teresio particularly liked the Japanese: He could not speak Japanese and that is why he ignored the tourist.

At last, Teresio saw him. A fiftyish man in a costly suit. Probably an automotive engineer. An American, Teresio hoped. It would be best were the man American.

"Interested in a good time tonight, sir?"

"Wadda have in mind, fella?"

Teresio could have jumped with joy. The man was American and was plastered-drunk.

"Girls. Your choice. Turin's best. One, I swear to you on Pope John's grave, she is a virgin. Pretty girls. They love Americans, I promise."

"Hold on, pal. Not so fast. How much?"

"You insult me. Did I mention money?"

"Listen, buddy, I know a proposition's gonna cost me when I hear it."

"This, my friend, is Turin. We are Italians. Hospitable people who like to party. What the cost is, that's up to you and the girls. But who worries about money when it's a good time?"

Teresio grasped the man by the arm and steered him into the service alley that ran behind a pair of gleamingly new first-class hotels. "Right this way, sir. It is close."

The man allowed Teresio to show him the way to the party. To the sexy Italian women. "These are clean girls, right?" Those were his last words before Teresio, sure that the empty alley afforded ample cover, brought the nine-inch pipe down hard on his head.

They actually do go out like a light, Teresio observed. The pipe had connected, and the man slumped wordlessly to the pavement. Teresio did not worry if the man was alive or dead.

It did not matter to him. What did matter is that the man's billfold held one hundred and five dollars. Teresio pocketed the cash, tossed the riffled billfold on the body, and skipped out of the alley. Yes, indeed—a party it would be. A $105-party tonight. And a $50 million-party starting tomorrow. The cash-flow picture had taken a decided turn for the better, Teresio found himself thinking. This time, he did not rebuke himself for using "sinister capitalisms." Somehow they struck him as appropriate. It was a good thing, Teresio decided, that he had studied economics. That would be a big help when it came time to invest the proceeds. A huge help.

"Go ahead. Talk to her, Lucky," Rod goaded as the men sat at the hotel bar and nursed a second beer. They awaited Stone's return from the doctor. The waiting was tense—it always is between battles, and the S-COM fighters smelled a second fight in the offing. They bantered and joked to kill the anxious time. That was the only amusement open to them. Myles, acting as Stone's second-in-command, had issued a three-drink rule, and he remained around to enforce it. Not that Rod and Lucky would have considered getting drunk. They knew their business too well to do that. But Myles, too, had no place to go, and in Stone's absence he felt obliged to offer whatever leadership was required.

Lucky eyed the girl Rod had indicated. A stewardess with blond hair, blue eyes, and evenly tanned skin. Based in Los Angeles, Lucky guessed, and miles from home with nothing to do in Turin. An attractive woman, there was no disputing.

Lucky could not resist a small dig at Rod. "Why not you, Rod! I swear, she's giving you the eye. Look at her, man. She's hot for you."

The girl's eyes looked nowhere near Rod. "Go on," he said sullenly. "She's not my type."

"If she's not your type, she sure is mine, my man. She sure is." Lucky strolled over to her and, to Rod's mounting jealousy, soon the two were merrily laughing and Lucky had bought her a drink.

Even though he resented Lucky's successes with women, Rod had to admire his work. Watch his style, Rod always told himself. It may work for me, too. It never did, but Rod kept on trying.

"Fookin' christ, Myles. The boy is fast."

"Why do you think he's called 'Lucky'?" Myles noted.

The two added the sport of Lucky-watching to their time killing regimen. It, too, helped the waiting—and helped it all the more since both would bet that this was one Lucky move that would not culminate in bed. Not for lack of trying on Lucky's part. Time, they figured, would run out. Action was nearing.

While Lucky was proving the truth behind his nickname, Stone, meantime, was having precisely the opposite kind of luck. DelRay was on the phone again.

"Williams, Turin is not the Wild West. You can't start shooting at every moving target. Not in my city, you can't."

"Chief," Stone calmly demurred, "those 'targets' were armed members of the Costello family. And that's a problem you won't—"

"I know who they were," DelRay angrily interrupted. "You got the boss, the *capo,* everybody. You wiped them out. But—"

Stone perceived the problem. "You know your job better than I do," Stone waxed politely. "But if I were you, I'd call every newspaper in town to announce the elimination of the Costello threat in Turin. A job very well done by the Turin police chief and his force, I'd say. Right now, I'd be holding a press conference. This is important news, Chief."

Stone swore he could *hear* DelRay's lips moving into a smile. "We do work well together, don't we?"

"Yes we do, Chief." Each word he pronounced made Stone hate even more intensely his need to lie, to butter up and smooth any ruffled feathers on the local law enforcement agents in towns where S-COM operated. He did not mind handing them the credit for S-COM successes: That benefited Stone as well. The shadows were more conducive to doing S-COM's work than were the bright glares of TV lights. But the limitless greed, for fame and cash alike, of police bureaucrats in every town Stone knew, that's what rankled him. Even so, he had to rein his ire tautly. S-COM routinely violated dozens of laws wherever it went. Homicide, illegal possession of firearms, wire tapping, assault: All carried felony charges, and S-COM curried the favor of local police chiefs to ensure that law enforcement right down the line to the beat cops looked the other way. Just one night in jail could wreck an S-COM timetable. Just one overeager beat cop could spell the fine margin between success and failure for an S-COM mission. That's why Stone held his tongue and his anger, and also held the hands of edgy, fumbling cops.

"Now, about the DiGrazia case . . ." DelRay was saying. That got to Stone. He had handed the chief $15,000 and a signed, sealed, and delivered Mafia bust, but DelRay wanted more. Still more. Stone's rising anger got the better of him.

"Let me tell you a fable, DelRay. I want you to listen very, very carefully. Once upon a time there was an Italian city. In that city there was a police chief. That chief thought himself pretty smart. His palm was always extended, and people put lots of cash in it. Mafia, security teams, everybody gave that chief money. He had a good thing going, this chief did. Then one day a foreigner came into his office and, sure enough, offered the chief money. The chief took it. That was a mistake. A *big* mistake. The foreigner, you see, had a tape recorder running throughout the transaction. On that tape you hear the snapping of crisp bills and the bargain that was struck. Later, the chief overplayed his hand. The foreigner got mad and he gave that tape to a big TV station. That was the end of the chief. Did you like my fable, Chief DelRay?"

DelRay said nothing.

"It *is* only a fable, chief, I want you to know. No one would pass along that tape if the police chief kept his end of the deal. That would be bad for business."

DelRay's uncharacteristic silence remained in force. Stone wished he could see his face. Bright red, Stone figured it would be. Stone nearly regretted doing this to DelRay. It was mean and, more importantly, unnecessary. But Stone rectified matters with DelRay, however, without diminishing in the remotest the cutting message of the fable.

"You asked me about the DiGrazia case, Chief. It will be solved by tomorrow. And, without your help, we never could have solved the case. The credit will all be yours."

Stone heard DelRay's breath returning to normal.

"Yes, Mr. Williams. Thank you. I would like that very much." DelRay rushed his words. "And we, of course, stand ready to offer any assistance you may need. Anything at all."

"Thanks, Chief. We'll be in touch," Stone said and started to hang up the receiver.

"Wait. Mr. Williams. About that fable—"

"Chief, it's only a story." Stone curtly broke the connection. He was glad that DelRay was inextricably in his pocket but more worried than ever about the fate of the DiGrazia girl.

"Mr. Williams?" DiGrazia burst in. The man's politeness, his unmarred dignity under these enormous pressures touched Stone. He wished he had solidly good news to relay. But he did not.

"We're down to the wire," Stone confessed candidly. A peak at his watch told Stone that Friday, Maria's final day, would soon be upon them. "We've a few more leads to check out. They're promising, but that's all. There are no assurances, Mr. DiGrazia. Not in this business."

"I know, Mr. Williams. I know. But isn't there something I can do? Anything?"

With time slipping away, DiGrazia was getting frantic. He controlled it well. Stone did not begrudge him his feelings. Were Stone in his position he had to admit he did not know how well he himself would tolerate the strain.

"As a matter of fact, Mr. DiGrazia, there is." Stone's mind sped down the list of remaining S-COM tasks; he found one to occupy DiGrazia. It was not make-work—DiGrazia, Stone sensed, would see right through that. "A little plan I have. A last resort to buy more time if necessary."

DiGrazia readily agreed to the plan Stone sketched. He admired Stone's ingenuity, and he busied himself following the S-COM leader's instructions. DiGrazia carefully bundled up stacks of bills—real bank notes on the outside; play money inside. One, two, three genuine bills at the front and back of the pile. A clump, ninety or so, of worthless pieces of paper within. Four suitcases were to be stuffed with this mixed tender: DiGrazia had his night's work cut out for him.

Stone smiled as he watched the vigor with which DiGrazia attacked his assignment. Stone hoped he would not have to put DiGrazia's work into play, that the suitcases would never be budged from Especiale. But if Friday rolls around and Maria DiGrazia still remains in the SMF hands, well—Stone thought no further as he walked away from DiGrazia. He would not permit himself to.

"Any changes, Stone?" Sophia Giacomo interrupted.

Stone's soft head shake told Sophia all the bad news she needed to know.

"You'll save her, Stone. I know you will."

"Thanks, Sophia, for the vote of confidence. And I'll tell you what. When we do save Maria, you and I will take a weekend vacation, eh?"

"I'll take you up on that, Stone. And it will be *this* weekend."

It had to be. Sophia and Stone both knew it was the coming weekend. Or none at all.

"You got it. A weekend trip to anywhere you choose."

"Anywhere." Sophia shyly giggled.

Stone enjoyed Sophia's company and enjoyed even more the images his mind conjured of a long, lazy, luxurious vacation with Sophia. But her question returned him to the deadliness of S-COM's mission. "Anywhere *out* of Italy. Anywhere at all."

Sophia got Stone's message. His thinking had snapped back to Maria and terrorism, and she left him to his last-minute mullings. But despite her strong and powerful fears for Maria, Stone's was a promise Sophia believed would be kept.

"Gina, what are you going to do this weekend?"

The question startled her. Gina had not thought past tomorrow, the day of what she was sure would be final reckoning. "Huh? Tomorrow?"

"A big date? What?" Maria insisted. She begged for a relief from the escalating tension in their shared cell. Talk, no matter how inappropriate to their desperate situation, afforded an escape valve. "What will you do next week?"

Gina searched for an answer. "It's strange, you know. It occurred to me that I gave up planning months ago. Seems like I've been drifting along, and now—" she gestured to their prison door, "I'm caught up in a bad current. Plans, I really have none. None at all."

"But, Gina, you're too young, too nice to live that way."

"For certain, Maria, whatever my plans hold, there'll be no more of this stuff. No more playing with guns and playing with revolution. It's odd, how I got into this. . . ."

Maria was absorbed by Gina's biography and how her concern for preserving Italy's art treasures abruptly became a nightmare. "I got it," Maria said when Gina's story reached its end. "You'll be the art director for Especiale. Papa's been thinking about hiring one, somebody to help make Especiales truly beautiful."

Gina allowed herself a laugh. "I don't think he'd hire me, Maria."

"You don't know Papa," Maria said, smiling.

"But I helped *kidnap* you, Maria."

"You were there, Gina. That's all. Your gun did not shoot, I remember. It made you sick. I remember that, too."

"But I was there."

"So? I'm glad for it. Who saved me from *him?*" Maria underlined her "him" with an angry gesture at Teresio's lair.

Gina could only smile at the innocence of her cellmate and the kindness of her dreams. That would be a dream, Gina knew: Lending her talents to transforming automobiles into art. It was possible, she conceded. It might even be fun. But it was all a dream, and real life does not have fairy-tale endings.

"Halt!" The order rang through the still night air. Leah was within one hundred yards of the suspected SMF hide-out. The sound came from behind her, from the direction of the hide-out. "Stop or I'll shoot."

Leah spun around cautiously as she fingered the trigger of her HK automatic pistol. But she could not afford a shoot-out, not on this street and not without S-COM backup. Maria DiGrazia's life could end with a single shot on the street. That might be ample to prod a fidgety terrorist into eliminating her.

Leah did not know what to expect when she turned to

face the man who had screamed the command. A mugger? A member of the SMF on sentry duty?

"Put those hands up high. Touch the moon."

It was a pair of Turin cops. Leah could only hope that the bellowed orders had not keyed a lethal chain of events that would culminate in Maria's murder. Leah obediently stretched her arms skyward.

"A prowler, that's what we have. Cover her and I'll frisk her."

"My name," Leah recited, "is Leah Aviv. An Israeli citizen. I am in the employ of Mr. Salvatore DiGrazia of Especiale."

"Yeah. Doing what?" one of the cops asked disbelievingly.

"Contract work," Leah responded ambiguously.

"Contract work? I'll bet. What's this?"

The cop withdrew the 9 mm pistol from Leah's shoulder holster. Seconds later he stumbled upon a double-edged, twelve-inch hunting knife that had been crafted for Leah by T.J. Wilson of Tacoma, Washington, the world's premier metal worker for night fighters.

"Contract work you said, lady? Explain the gun and the knife to the desk sergeant."

Leah mumly let him cuff her. She had weighed the odds. Escaping from these Turin cops would not have been the problem: A flick of a shuriken at the cop who covered her would have neutralized him; a quick kick and a chop or two would put the other one on the ground. But the one with the drawn pistol might have managed a shot. Leah did not fear for her own safety; she feared for Maria DiGrazia's. Leah compliantly entered the patrol car for the ride to the station. A few phone calls, Leah figured, and she would be free within thirty minutes, an hour at most. It was the better gamble.

"Should I call the police?"

"What? Are you mad?" The manager stared at his assistant. "*This* is Balducci's."

"But *that*—" the assistant pointed exasperatedly, "is a shoplifter. I remember him. From the other night, when the woman, poor Signora Albanese—"

"Say no more. I do not wish to remember. If he steals tonight, call the police. Otherwise do nothing. Do you hear me? *Nothing*. That is our policy. These disturbances. . . ." The manager's voice trailed off into unhappy memories of the miserable night when Signora Albanese had been robbed right within the store. That was the horror to him: That it happened in Balducci's.

Teresio strolled the sprawling and crammed aisles of Balducci's oblivious to the watchful eyes of the assistant manager. The bountiful displays of cheeses, wines, pastries, and sausages won his rapt attention. He busied himself shoveling goodies into his cart. This was a pleasure: grocery *shopping*. Teresio fondled each delicacy that he gently placed into his cart. A round of provolone here; a salami there; a bit of mortadella; a loaf of bread and a battle of fresh olive oil—and hang the price, Teresio thought. Some ground coffee and a little espresso pot; he hoped that old camping stove still worked.

"Excuse me. Where's the Moët White Star champagne?"

The question enraged the assistant manager. He remembered Teresio and his last bottle of Moët. "Over there," he said as he sullenly pointed to a cooler and, in a flash, determined there was no way this scruffy character could pay for the mountain of groceries he was accumulating. The question about Moët corked it. He stalked off to phone the police.

Two bottles of Moët added to the heap in Teresio's cart. A few vegetables—a tomato and a quart of green olives—completed the shopping list. Teresio mentally added up the bill and shoved off to the cash register.

"That will be ninety-eight dollars and fifty-six cents, sir."

The assistant manager watched the scene unfold. He *knew* this troublemaker would pick up a few of his groceries—the champagne certainly—and bolt for the door without paying. That's when he would get a surprise, a big one. The assistant manager smiled in satisfaction.

His smile turned first to a frown and then to a look of complete consternation. "Ten, twenty, thirty, . . ." With each bill the troublemaker counted out, the assistant manager's bewilderment grew. He stood frozen to his vigilant post.

Teresio paid in full. Only six bucks left, he noted to himself, but come the morning, that would all change, so he might as well celebrate his looming success. Teresio hoisted his bags and walked out of Balducci's in anticipation of the merry night to come.

"Freeze!"

"Oh my God," Teresio exclaimed to himself when he saw the cop's pointed gun. "Good fucking Christ, the deal is over." He dropped his laden grocery bags to the sidewalk and—he could hear his plump tomatoes squishing—lifted his hands.

"It's a horrible mistake. Horrible. How can we make it up to you? I'm sorry, officers. You can go now. It's all been a misunderstanding," the assistant manager whined obsequiously.

"Here, let me help you with your bags. Wait. Your tomatoes, they're squashed. Hold on. Just one second."

The assistant manager dashed into the store and speedily returned with a half-dozen tomatoes and a chilled bottle of Moët's Dom Perignon, the apex of the champagne line. "Please accept this. We welcome our valued customers. I am so sorry."

Teresio could not be angry. Relief that his scam was not over bathed him. He did not understand this man's babbling, but he understood champagne; and no matter why, any store that hands out free bottles of Dom Perignon is okay by Teresio. "Balducci's will always get my business," Teresio reassured the employee sincerely before walking away.

The baffled assistant manager returned to his post. It made no sense. But he did not have long to ponder that bewildering interlude. The manager shortly gave him a new thought to mull.

"The Dom Perignon. It is forty-five dollars the bottle. Add two for the tomatoes. That's forty-seven dollars. It comes out of your paycheck. I told you, this is Balducci's."

When Stone returned to the hotel, the clock read 12:30 A.M. Friday, Maria DiGrazia's last day, had begun. There was no message from Leah; he assumed her mission had produced no consequential evidence. And it was late. Stone put in wake-up calls for every S-COM member for 4:30 A.M. and promptly fell fast asleep.

Like Stone, Lucky was in his room and in bed. Unlike Stone, Lucky did not think of sleep. He thought only of Morgan. That was her name, and Lucky's barroom guess was right, she did work as a stewardess. He moved fast, Lucky did. Two hours after first approaching Morgan, there still was no word from Stone about a night operation, so Lucky had proposed his own night operation and Morgan eagerly agreed.

Lucky loved love; he loved to make love. His lips started at Morgan's mouth and slowly worked their way down every inch of her tanned body. Morgan's mouth reciprocated. She, too, was ready for love and happy to have this pleasant Cuban interlude in what otherwise would have been a boring, lonely layover night.

Morgan's mouth enveloped Lucky's erection and slowly excited him. His hands roamed delicately across the entirety of her long, thin body; his fingers lingered on her breasts as her head bobbed faster and faster. His hips rose and fell in synchronization with her erotic rhythm. He felt himself ejaculating, hot and fast, into her waiting mouth. But she uninterruptedly maintained her sucking rhythm and his erection returned. When she felt him hardening, Morgan lifted her mouth and gradually kissed her way up Lucky's body until their faces met; she mounted him adroitly and slid him into her.

Lucky liked the amorous change of pace: He grabbed Morgan's ass and thrust himself higher and deeper into her. Dozens, even hundreds of times their pelvises embraced. He relaxed when he heard Morgan climaxing and felt himself ejaculating into her again.

They kissed more, and began the preparatory steps to lovemaking again. But a fleeting and accidental glance at his watch brought Lucky back from this amorous dreamland to the realities of Turin. "Shit, Morgan, it's 2:30."

"So?" She kissed his neck oblivious to the lateness of the hour; oblivious, in fact, to everything but the immediacy of their romance.

"So, indeed!" Lucky said. He climbed back into Morgan, where he would remain until his wake-up call put a halt to their reveries. But Lucky knew the morning's call would come early, and he knew he would have to be ready. He was young; he would be ready. Lucky was a professional: He *always* had to be ready.

"Fuck, this Moët is good, damn good," Teresio slurped as he drained the second bottle of White Star and uncorked the precious Dom Perignon. "Save the best for last, that's what I always say." He was drunk, he recognized, but he wanted to party even if he was alone. He laughed as he nibbled at the last of the cheese and sausages: His prisoners in the closet had to be starving and here he was gorging himself. "But screw 'em. Ain't no Geneva Convention for kidnappers. Or their prisoners. I make the rules here," he proudly reminded himself.

"Shit, I'm drunk." Teresio hiked the Dom Perignon high and rapidly chugged a third of the bottle. "Damn good stuff, it is. But, wow, I'm shit-faced." He thought again of the dark, roach-infested loneliness of his hungry prisoners. "What do I care? Fuck 'em." The idea hit home: That is exactly what he wanted to do. "Fuck 'em. I mean, I'll fuck the DiGrazia bitch. That's what she needs, a good lay and I am in *the* mood to give it to her."

Teresio's head danced as he paced the distance to the girls' closet-cell. He swilled the last of the Dom Perignon, smacked his lips, and unlocked the door.

"Get the fuck out of here, Vincent," Gina commanded menacingly. "You're drunk. Get out!"

"Aw shut your hole, bitch." To punctuate his order, Teresio swung the Dom Perignon bottle down hard on her head. Glass flew everywhere; Gina slumped unconsciously to the floor. Blood trickled from her forehead, Maria saw. Then she felt Teresio's hands yanking her out of the closet. She could only imagine what her fate would be now, and none of the pictures in her mind were pretty ones.

"You rich bitches are all alike, you know that?" Teresio slurred. "Over here." He dragged Maria along the floor by her hair. It hurt, but Maria feared Teresio—his madness and his drunkeness—far too much to scream in pain or in protest of his roughness.

Teresio tossed her on the mattress, untied her leg and hand bindings, lifted an AK-47 in the air and pointed its barrel straight at Maria. "Take off your skirt," he commanded. Maria grabbed instead for the other AK-47, the one that had been Gina's. With a finger on the trigger, she aimed the gun at Teresio. He responded by laughing. "Pull the trigger, shithead. Tug it!" Images of death, blood, and the murder of her bodyguards clouded Maria's mind. The AK-47 sickened her. But she squeezed the trigger desperately. She squeezed harder. She squeezed a third time. Nothing happened. No bullets roared out of the barrel.

"Fucking cunt. You would have killed me! Dumb bitch. There's no magazine in the gun," Teresio howled with drunken laughter. He reached over and tore off Maria's skirt. "No bullets, no bang bang!"

Maria saw Teresio's smile disappear. "Take off those white panties, bitch, and spread 'em."

Maria dropped the useless AK-47 and moved her hands to the elastic band that held her panties in place. But she could not do it; she would never stoop to his insanely animalistic level. She had never been naked with a man in this way, and she would not spoil the loves she would have by letting this be her first, no matter what.

"No! I will not. Kill me, you pig, but you cannot make me make love with you," Maria insisted. Nor would she let herself cry before this demented man, although that was exactly what she wanted to do: allow her tears of rage, frustration, and despair to roll down her cheeks. But she would not give him that satisfaction. "You pig!"

"Who's the pig, whore? And you *are* going to screw before the night is over," Teresio swore. His gun never lost its aim at her. "You won't take off your panties? Big deal. I'll do it for you."

As Teresio's left hand grabbed Maria's underpants and tugged, his right hand kept a steady grip on his weapon's trigger. Maria considered for a second trying to wrest the gun away, but she lost her nerve and, in that moment of indecision, lost her panties, too. She squeezed her legs tightly together to cover her nakedness. Teresio just laughed.

"Smile big!"

The glimpse of Maria's brownly lush pubic region undid Teresio. He came in his pants. "Wider!" He poked the AK-47 barrel between her legs, and his excitement mounting, his penis drained itself of semen. "This is going to be fun," Teresio muttered. He dropped his pants to the floor and stood naked before Maria. He maintained his grip on the gun.

But Teresio's spent penis remained shriveled. "Your bra—take it off," Teresio commanded. One look at those large breasts would restore him, Teresio ardently believed.

Her fear escalating, Maria slipped out of her bra. Her breasts fell free; their whiteness starkly contrasted with the bronze tone of the rest of her body.

Teresio's breath panted. He could feel Maria around him, feel himself smothering her in lust. Get bigger, he demanded of his penis. Its moist, wilted head mocked him: His penis nonchalantly disobeyed his order.

Maria stared at Teresio's body, at his relaxed penis. She knew, despite her virginity, that something was amiss. She began to feel that there might be a way out, that there might be an escape from this repugnant man and his sadism.

Teresio's anger soared in step with Maria's optimism. He cursed himself for ejaculating so soon, for swilling three bottles of champagne, for messing up the night he had long planned. But the evening meant too much for him: He was not surrendering so easily. His brain drunkenly stumbled through the possibilities. But, with each passing moment, he felt the effects of the champagne increasing. It had been a very long time since Teresio had last treated himself to a single bottle of champagne; he could not recollect if he had ever before drunk three whole bottles at a single sitting. His mind reeled; he tried to shake the alcoholic fog away.

An erection, Teresio told himself, that's what he needed. He stared at his penis: Its smallness laughed at him. Teresio considered the possibilities. He could force Maria to make him large again; the gun would goad her into using her mouth or hands to restore his hardness. But no, no, Teresio reminded himself. He painfully thought of how hard Maria had squeezed his testicles when he approached her the last time. She would squeeze them again or, worse still, bite through his erection, Teresio fretted.

He saw only one thing left to do. He pointed the gun at Maria's mouth. "I'm coming to take your cherry," he drunkenly cackled—and with that, he clicked on the safety and threw himself between Maria's legs.

She struggled. Her hands pulled his hair. Teresio slapped her face. Maria tried to knee him in the groin, but she missed and the blow thunked into Teresio's abdomen. She could feel his superior strength, but she could tell, too, that Teresio's drunkeness had deprived him of coordination. Half his punches and slaps landed wide of their mark; the others slammed into her impotently.

If only she could knock him out, Maria prayed, this whole dismal nightmare would end. Forever. She mustered all her power into a single blow aimed at Teresio's nose. Her tiny fist connected; Teresio's nose flattened against his face. Blood gushed out of the nostrils and poured down his face. He shrieked in agony; Teresio felt blackness enveloping him. He swung his elbow with all his might at Maria's forehead. It smacked on target.

Both fell, nakedly and heavily, to the mattress. Unconsciousness engulfed them.

"A telephone call. I want to make my one phone call," Leah announced to the Turin Police Station's night-watch commander.

He roared with amusement. "Lady, you think this is, what's it called, *Kojak?* Your phone call!" He laughed even harder at his joke. "It's 2:00 A.M. You cannot get out on bail until a judge hears the charges against you."

"When," Leah demanded to know, "will that be?"

"In the morning at the earliest. Maybe Monday. Depends on when a judge is available. Until then, don't you worry. We'll give you a home."

The commander chuckled again; Leah sizzled at his cruel humor. "My phone call, then. Where's a phone?"

"I told you. It's late. You can call in the morning. Don't worry,"—the commander sized up Leah's athletically trim body—"we'll find ways to keep you busy."

Leah struggled to check her anger. She knew she had to get out of the police station quickly: Maria's life might depend on how soon S-COM freed her. But she knew as well that she could not divulge the true nature of her midnight mission to the watch commander. S-COM policy on that point was firm: Police were told only the barest minimum that they absolutely needed to know. Otherwise, S-COM would be courting disaster by inviting the fumbling assistance of local gendarmes. But a night in this Turin jail, that would be a disaster, too. For Maria DiGrazia.

"I want to make my call. To Police Chief DelRay."

The watch commander howled: "Why not the Pope?"

Minutes more of this banter ate away at the clock. The watch commander, however, became increasingly unsure of himself. His face told Leah that he was growing concerned that perhaps his obstinate refusal to accommodate her would cost him his job.

Leah unveiled a new ploy. "Stone Williams. Do you know him? Have you heard of him?"

"Who?"

"Stone Williams. Or perhaps you've heard of the Costello family. What *used* to be the Costello family, that is."

The watch commander's smiling face froze. "That phone call. You said Chief DelRay?"

Now Leah smiled; the watch commander's expression had shifted to a nervous frown.

Leah considered changing her order to a call to Stone. But that would waste more time, she decided. Stone would have to call DelRay, and DelRay in turn would call the Police Station. Calling DelRay himself was the most direct route, and that's the one Leah always preferred. "Yes, DelRay."

"But it's 3:00," the watch commander sniveled. "It could mean my job to call the chief at this hour. I'll be back on the beat."

"Mister, it will mean *more* than your job if you *don't* call."

The watch commander's eyes took Leah's measure: The stern cast to her face; the toughness of her body. He thought of her weapons—they were not the usual tools of burglars and muggers.

He put in the call.

CHAPTER 10

"Stone! Wake up," Leah hollered as she insistently pounded on her commander's door. "Wake up! It's me, Leah."

Stone greeted her groggily. "What time is it? What's up, Leah?"

It took Stone a few seconds to shake his sleep off, but Leah's report on her nocturnal activities speeded up the process. "Fucking DelRay and his cops," Stone allowed himself to curse before turning his full concentration on the mission that lay urgently before S-COM. It was 3:50, Friday morning, when Leah finished her report.

"We'll strike at dawn. In two hours. Round up the troops. I want full combat dress and equipment. We'll throw everything into this. It's our only move. If the SMF is holed up in that building, we'll blow them to Rome and back again if we have to. You wake up the men, Leah. I have a call to make."

Leah exited to awaken Myles, Rod, and Lucky—and she wondered why a mischievous smile had crossed Stone's face.

"Chief DelRay," Stone bellowed into his mouthpiece. "Yes, I know it's four in the morning. Of course I know about that unfortunate incident with Leah Aviv. You're sorry, I know."

"A thousand apologies, Mr. Williams," DelRay bleated into his telephone.

"Look, chief, I'm calling because I need you for a big

mission . . . a *very* sensitive job, and you're the best man for it. It will be crucial to solving the DiGrazia case, I can promise you. I need you to stake out the site where the ransom will be dropped. Right, right. You got it." Stone gave DelRay the address. "The important thing, chief, is you have to get there fast. Right now. In a few hours, Mr. DiGrazia will personally deliver the money there. But we need surveillance starting right now to make certain it's not a trap. You'll do it yourself? Great! I knew I could count on you, chief. Just wait at the site until the kidnappers arrive to pick up the ransom. It could take hours, but it will be worth the wait. You know that. Oh, and chief, if the kidnappers do not show, why don't you keep the ransom money. You know, as a token of appreciation from me. Thanks, chief."

Stone hung up before DelRay could question him. He had to laugh. He would spare DiGrazia a trip out to the site until much later in the day. But this diversion would remove DelRay from S-COM's hair and, better still, pay him back for the miscues the chief and his men had inflicted on S-COM from the start. Stone reckoned there would be no more than three thousand real dollars in those piles of worthless play money, but it would take DelRay days to sort out the good from the bad. It was an expensive joke, but Stone applauded himself. If he, Leah, and his men could get no sleep tonight, Stone was damned if DelRay could. And now he could not. Stone slapped his hands together and started to dress for war.

Leah awakened Myles and Rod with a warning announcement at their doors. That was essential with men who slept with loaded guns at their sides. And she followed up by slipping her passkey into the lock and opening the door a crack to make sure the drowsy soldiers were indeed rising. It was early, and the mission was urgent. There was no time for mistakes.

"Lucky! It's Leah. Wake up!" Leah announced at Lucky's door and rapidly worked her key to gain entrance. Lucky slid out of Morgan just as Leah walked in.

"Sorry for the interruption," Leah said, blushing. "But duty calls."

"Only getting my morning exercise," Lucky joked.

Leah hurried from Lucky's room. She was satisfied that he was at least wide awake.

"Exercise! That's all I am to you," Morgan protested. She angrily slipped into her dress, tossed her panties into her purse, and rushed barefoot to the door.

"Don't forget your shoes," Lucky reminded her with a broad smile on his face.

Morgan huffed and returned to the bedside to retrieve them. Lucky grabbed her and planted a kiss on her lips. "It was good, Morgan."

She laughed. "Yes it was."

"Bye, Morgan. See you in Miami or New York sometime."

"Sometime, Lucky."

"But not now. Duty calls, you heard. See you."

"Later," Morgan said, then slipped out of the room.

The bright glare of the dawning sun snuck through the cracks in Teresio's boarded-up windows. He stirred, and his hand brushed Maria DiGrazia's bare breasts. That woke him with a start. "Fuck," Teresio shouted. The noise hurt his head; his hangover throbbed. He dimly remembered last night. His hand moved to his nose. Blood caked his face, and the slightest touch on his nose sent pain cascading through his body.

Maria DiGrazia moved slightly, enough for Teresio to notice. He pulled her hair, startling her out of the vestiges of sleep. "Bitch! You did this to me." Teresio indicated his battered nose. "You'll pay for that—and pay big." He spat out each word in that dark promise.

But not now, Teresio advised himself. Not now. He had too much to do. His face had to be cleaned up before setting out on busy streets to collect his fifty million. Guns had to be inspected to guard against possible mistakes. Too much to do to rape Maria now. Later, after the fifty million was safely pocketed, then there would be time aplenty to have Maria—and to kill her and Gina before setting out from Italy. The day's agenda brightened his face: This Friday was going to be the best day in Teresio's life.

He dragged Maria over to the closet and hurled her in. She landed with a thud on Gina. "Enjoy yourself while you can, girls," Teresio sneered as he locked the door tight.

"Gina, Gina! Are you alive?"

Gina's nodding head proved that she was. "How about you? Did he—" Gina hesitated to use the foul word, "were you raped?"

"No. No, I don't know exactly what happened. But I'm okay. My head hurts." She rubbed her forehead where Teresio's elbow had landed its knockout blow.

"Mine, too," Gina laughed and pointed to the blood-encrusted spot on her forehead where the champagne bottle had broken. "Watch out for glass."

"Ouch! I'm sitting on a piece."

Maria and Gina simultaneously broke into laughter, and their laughter soon was transformed into tears. They hugged each other. The end, they knew, was nearing.

Neither girl heard the miniscule sounds on the street below. Nor did Teresio; he was occupied with reassembling his AK-47. The gun was in perfect working order, and he counted over three hundred rounds on hand. Not that he expected to need more than two: One for Gina and the second for Maria. A quick flight to Geneva to open an account in a Swiss bank, and whoosh, he would be safely on his way to Los Angeles before the bodies were discovered. Not that he feared even a shred of evidence would be found that would connect him to the crime. Nor, certainly, would there be witnesses. Teresio would be in Fat City and would never have to look back.

Down on the street, Stone had accepted Leah's plan and was swiftly implementing it. Leah knew the layout better than Stone, and he also knew Leah had a high personal stake in freeing Maria DiGrazia. She had volunteered for the toughest assignment, too. Stone, despite his protective instincts regarding her, accepted that offer as well.

But time was now of the essence. Myles scampered to the back of the building and took aim with his HK MP5 at the second floor, the one that lay behind the boarded-up windows. Rod and Lucky each took a side. Stone took the front. None of the men sought protective cover. They stood boldly on the ground, there MP5s pointed high.

"Hard and fast," Stone had exhorted before sending his men off to their posts. "Nonstop firing until ceasefire arrives. I don't care how many are inside. I want to let them know they're going to be wiped out—and I want their attention focused on the street. Don't give them a second to think."

"You mean, nuke 'em, boss?" Rod had smiled when he heard the orders.

"*After* the DiGrazia girl is out, we just might, Rod." Stone thought for the last time of the little Turin girl whose face had been mangled in the Turin Post Office explosion. "We just might nuke 'em."

"You got it, boss." Rod had understood Stone's caveat. The DiGrazia girl had to come out alive. But that remained in Leah's hands. She had precisely three minutes by Stone's clock.

The positions had been assumed. Stone watched his clock. He granted everybody an extra thirty seconds: There could be no slip-ups.

"Fire!" Stone roared, and his MP5 led off a blisteringly hot chorus of S-COM guns. Stone let rip with one thirty-bullet magazine. Another followed. Then a third. Within ninety seconds, the ground about him was littered with spent magazines and bullet casings. He saw the boarded-up window above him, his target, giving way into a myriad splinters. He shoved in yet another magazine to finish his work.

Stone heard the gunfire from both sides and the building's rear. He heard no answering shots from within; that did not surprise him. Success of the S-COM plan hinged upon a stunning first-strike capability. Stone continued to flood the disintegrating boards with bullets. Then he heard a roar from inside the building. One gun only. An automatic, probably one of the AK-47s he had seen in DiGrazia's film, Stone figured. He realized anxiously that he did not know in which direction the AK-47 bullets were aimed. He fired off his MP5 rounds faster still, trying by the energy of his personal assault to win the terrorist's attention.

Stone's persistence paid off. The AK-47 barrel poked through the hole where the window above Stone had been. Its bullets zinged wildly in Stone's direction. The terrorist within was shooting blindly. He was afraid, Stone could tell, and too fearful to venture a look at the street below him.

Stone answered the terrorist's fire with more rounds of his own. He had already shot several hundred rounds, but he kept at his steady pace. Thirty-seconds more and all S-COM firing ceased. Stone watched his second hand move as the trigger finger on his right hand maintained its steady flow of bullets.

"Time! Ceasefire!" Stone shouted. S-COM, as always, was precise: His oral order was unnecessary. Each man had been watching his time. All firing from the street stopped, and an eerie silence replaced the battle noises. All of them except the sputtering of the terrorist's AK-47. Stone gave him fifteen more seconds to shoot. Then it would be over. *If* the plan worked. Stone's heart beat fast as Myles, Rod, and Lucky joined him in front. Anxiety read on every face.

But not on Leah's. At that moment, she was as calm as a lake on a windless afternoon. She could climb the Alps, she had told Stone, and she definitely could scale a two-story building.

"The Alps don't shoot back," Stone had retorted. But in the end, he adopted her plan—and now it was up to Leah. She knew Maria DiGrazia's life was in her hands as she inched her way up the building to the second floor. Leah moved sure-footedly up the building. Its old bricks provided sufficient footholds for a trained mountaineer.

Leah silently lifted her face to where a side window had been. Rod's pinpoint firing had done its job: Every board was ripped into bits. Leah could see the terrorist—only one, she surprisedly noted; S-COM had expected two—firing down at Stone's position. This was the crucial moment. Leah's time was up. The S-COM firing had ceased.

Leah hurled herself through the window and, in a continuous somersault, landed on her feet two yards inside the hide-out. The terrorist turned to face the intruder. But, simultaneous with the touchdown of her feet, Leah had released a shuriken. It whizzed through the air. She removed her pistol for insurance and could hear Stone and the troops rushing the stairs. The terrorist pointed his AK-47 at Leah.

The shuriken struck; it sliced into his windpipe. Leah holstered her gun while he slumped to the floor and gasped for air.

Stone kicked in the door and S-COM burst in. Stone surveyed the scene and smiled. "She's here. That's our man. Find the girl."

Rod was the first to notice the closet, and his huge foot smashed powerfully into the door—the wood, lock, and frame gave way to his assault. He heard crying from within as he bullishly pulled the rest of the door down. "Poor baby," Rod said softly. "It's all right now. You're safe. It's over."

Maria DiGrazia hugged Rod and screamed and cried and laughed and kissed him. Embarrassed, he struggled with words until he noticed another body in the closet. "Hey, boss. There's a second one in there." Rod reached in and lifted Gina out. "Are you okay?" Rod asked. "It's fine now. Everything will be fine."

Stone's sharp eyes picked out the second girl instantly. He knew Teresio from his body build, and he recognized this girl from the kidnapping film, too. The body and the T-shirt were the same: Mona Lisa smiled out at them all. Gina just sobbed.

"There, there," Rod mothered Gina. "Tell us who you are now." Gina cried harder as visions of barren and hostile prison cells paraded before her eyes.

"She's my friend," Maria said. "My friend."

"What about him?" Stone gestured toward Teresio.

Maria shrieked at her first sight of the bleeding, gasping Teresio. "He's the one. He kidnapped me. Him!"

"Alone," Stone probed. "He did it all by himself?"

Maria did not hesitate. "Yes. By himself." Then she joined Gina in crying, and the two liberated captives hugged each other.

"Let's get a move on," Stone commanded. "Mr. Di-

Grazia is waiting. And I'm sure you can't wait to see him, Maria. Where do you want to go, Miss," Stone politely inquired of Gina.

"With me. She's coming with me," Maria answered.

Stone did not understand the picture. But he got it. He was not a policeman. Guilt and innocence before the bar were abstractions to him. Guilt and innocence in the field, the war rules, that's what Stone believed in. And Stone could imagine no judge better positioned than Maria DiGrazia to mete out justice in this case. If Maria stuck by her resolve to keep "Mona Lisa"—as Stone nicknamed Gina—out of it, Stone would not stand in the way. Only the film of the kidnapping could link "Mona Lisa" to the crimc, and Stone had those reels. A match would put an end to that evidence.

But, Stone recalled, Teresio remained. "Rod—" No, Stone interrupted himself. He relished the rare moments when Rod's tenderness emerged. He would not disturb Rod in his doting on the two freed women. "Lucky, you stay here and mop up."

As S-COM and its two charges walked down the street, a single shot rang out from the building. Lucky came running after his comrades.